SCARED TO TRY AGAIN

With a loud caw, the crow launched itself into the air and circled above the riders.

Patch, who had just reached the first fence, was startled by the sudden noise and motion. Instead of jumping up and forward, he wheeled around and shied sideways, crashing into the fence. Scared even more by the impact, he reared up and twisted around, ending up straddling the remains of the jump. Merrill had barely managed to keep her seat and was clinging to Patch's mane, her stirrups swinging free of her feet. Max was already hurrying forward to catch the panicky horse, but Patch was too quick for him. He reared again, unseating Merrill completely, then darted away as the girl tumbled off and landed hard on her backside.

THE SADDLE CLUB

YANKEE SWAP

BONNIE BRYANT

A BANTAM SKYLARK BOOK
NEW YORK • TORONTO • LONDON • SYDNEY • AUCKLAND

I would like to express my special thanks to Catherine Hapka for her help in the writing of this book.

RL 5, 009–012

YANKEE SWAP

A Skylark Book / January 1996

Skylark Books is a registered trademark of Bantam Books, a division of Bantam Doubleday Dell Publishing Group, Inc. Registered in U.S. Patent and Trademark Office and elsewhere.

"The Saddle Club" is a registered trademark of Bonnie Bryant Hiller. The Saddle Club design/logo, which consists of a riding crop and a riding hat, is a trademark of Bantam Books.

"USPC" and "Pony Club" are registered trademarks of the United States Pony Clubs, Inc., at The Kentucky Horse Park, 4071 Iron Works Pike, Lexington, KY 40511-8462.

ISBN 0-553-48268-8

Published simultaneously in the United States and Canada

Bantam Books are published by Bantam Books, a division of Bantam Doubleday Dell Publishing Group, Inc. Its trademark, consisting of the words "Bantam Books" and the portrayal of a rooster, is Registered in U.S. Patent and Trademark Office and in other countries. Marca Registrada. Bantam Books, 1540 Broadway, New York, New York 10036.

PRINTED IN THE UNITED STATES OF AMERICA

OPM 0 9 8 7 6 5 4

1

"OH, THERE YOU ARE!" Lisa Atwood exclaimed. She looked up as her two best friends, Stevie Lake and Carole Hanson, hurried across the indoor ring to join her. It was Saturday morning, and that meant it was time for their Pony Club meeting. All three girls rode together at Pine Hollow Stables and belonged to Horse Wise, Pine Hollow's branch of the United States Pony Club.

"Hi, Lisa," Carole and Stevie said in one voice. Lisa was leaning against the wall, waiting for the meeting to start.

"Where the heck have you guys been?" Lisa asked, smiling so that they knew she wasn't really annoyed. "I thought I was going to be the only member of The Saddle Club to show up for Horse Wise today!"

Now they knew Lisa was kidding. None of the girls would

miss a Pony Club meeting unless there was a major emergency. The three friends loved riding more than anything. In fact, they loved it so much that they had formed The Saddle Club, which was dedicated to horses and riding and friends. The club had only two rules: Members had to be horse crazy, and they had to be willing to help out the others in any way necessary.

"I was a little late today," Carole explained. "My dad had to make a few phone calls before he dropped me off, and it took him longer than he thought."

"And what about you, young lady?" Lisa asked, turning to Stevie with mock sternness. "You know it's very important for riders to be prompt."

Stevie and Carole laughed. They knew that Lisa was imitating Max Regnery, the owner of Pine Hollow and the girls' riding instructor. The Saddle Club liked Max a lot, and they knew he was an excellent teacher. Still, they couldn't help poking fun at his strictness once in a while.

"If you must know, I have a very good excuse for being late," Stevie informed Lisa loftily. "I was helping Max roll the bandages for today's lesson. I even got here early."

Carole raised an eyebrow in surprise. "Really?" she said. "That was awfully helpful of you, Stevie." All the young riders at Pine Hollow were expected to help out with a wide variety of stable chores in addition to taking care of the horses they rode. Stevie was willing to do her share, but her friends knew that she usually preferred it if her share happened to take place a little later in the day.

Before Carole could open her mouth to tease Stevie, Lisa

broke in. "Well, never mind—you're both here now and that's what counts. I've been dying to tell you my great news. Remember hearing me talk about my friend Merrill?"

Carole nodded. "The one who lives in Maine, right?"

"That's right," Lisa said. "Well, guess what? Her school has an extra winter break because it's always so cold there this time of year, so her parents said she could come visit me!"

"She's coming here?" Stevie said. "That's great!"

"I know," Lisa said. "I haven't seen her in a couple of years. But that's not even the best part. The best part is that I've written to her so much about Pine Hollow that she finally decided to try riding herself about six months ago, and she loves it."

"That's great," Stevie said again, but Lisa noticed that her friend looked a little distracted. She followed Stevie's gaze and saw that another member of Horse Wise had just sauntered in—Veronica diAngelo. Veronica was a spoiled rich girl who cared more about what she wore than how she rode. In fact, her attitude had gotten her kicked out of Horse Wise more than once, though Max always let her back in after she behaved herself for a while.

Lisa didn't know why Stevie was paying so much attention to Veronica, but she was too excited to care. Merrill was one of her favorite people, and she hadn't seen her in ages. She couldn't wait to introduce her to the rest of The Saddle Club and to show her Pine Hollow, especially now that Merrill was an enthusiastic rider, too.

"How wonderful, Lisa," Carole said. "We'll take her on lots of trail rides. How long is she staying?"

"She's coming next Friday, staying the whole following week, and leaving Sunday," Lisa said. "She's got some relatives who live around here, so she'll have plenty to do while I'm in school." She sighed. "I just wish *my* school were on break then, too. That way Merrill and I could spend even more time riding together."

"Well, after school and weekends is definitely better than nothing. I wonder which horse she should ride while she's here," Carole said thoughtfully. "If she's been riding six months she's probably already too advanced for Patch or Nero. How good do you think she is?"

Lisa burst out laughing. "I haven't even seen her in years," she exclaimed. "How do you expect me to give you a detailed report on her riding ability?"

Carole looked a little hurt. "Well, she must write about it in her letters . . ."

"Sorry," Lisa said. "I know you're only trying to help." She shook her head, still smiling. "I can just picture it—you're going to be the perfect riding instructor and stable manager someday."

Carole's life plans were well known to her friends. She was definitely going to do something involving horses. She wasn't sure yet whether that meant she would be a trainer, an instructor, a competitive rider, a vet, or all of the above.

Stevie finally turned her attention away from Veronica and back to the conversation. "So what does she say in her letters?" she asked Lisa. "Is she a good rider?"

Lisa shrugged. "Actually, it's a little hard to tell," she admitted. "Merrill doesn't blow her own horn, if you know what I mean. She says she's still a beginner, but she's starting to jump, so she must be doing okay."

Carole was about to ask another question when her thoughts were interrupted by giggles from nearby. She turned toward the door and saw two more members of Horse Wise, Betsy Cavanaugh and Adam Levine, enter together. Betsy was hanging on Adam's arm and gazing at him admiringly, giggling madly at something he was saying.

"Oh, gag," Stevie commented. "It looks like Betsy has another new love interest." Betsy was a pretty, lively, friendly girl. She was also becoming known as the stable flirt.

"Poor Joe," Carole said. "I guess he's been dumped." Joe Novick was the best-looking boy in Horse Wise and, last Carole had heard, Betsy's boyfriend.

"Try to keep up, Carole," Stevie said, rolling her eyes. "Betsy and Joe broke up weeks ago. Last I heard, she was dating someone at school."

Lisa glanced over at Betsy and Adam. "I would have thought Adam was too sensible to fall for Betsy's flirting."

"Me too," Stevie said. A devilish look crossed her face. "Hey, Adam!" she called out. "You'd better watch out! Delilah will be jealous if she sees you talking to another woman." Delilah was the mare Adam had been riding in class lately.

Adam laughed self-consciously, but Betsy rolled her eyes, barely bothering to glance in Stevie's direction. "I think some people around here need to grow up a little," she commented loudly to Adam. "Maybe then they'd see there's more to life than just horses."

Stevie scowled. "For your information, Betsy, I—"

"Horse Wise, come to order!" Max's voice interrupted Stevie's retort. Max stood at the front of the group with his mother, universally known as Mrs. Reg, at his side.

Stevie perked up again immediately. "Time for bandaging practice," she said eagerly.

Lisa and Carole exchanged puzzled glances. It wasn't like Stevie to get so excited about what was a necessary—but fairly boring—lesson.

"Before we get started on today's activity, I have a very special announcement," Max said.

Carole and Lisa immediately forgot all about Stevie and bandages. Max's "very special announcements" were almost always about something exciting at Pine Hollow.

"Beginning next week, I'll be . . ." Max's voice trailed off, and he frowned a little. "Betsy, Adam," he said sternly. "May I have your attention please?"

Betsy and Adam immediately stopped whispering. Adam's face turned bright red, and Betsy gave Max an apologetic smile.

"Serves them right," Stevie muttered. "This is a Horse Wise meeting, not a dating service."

"As I was saying," Max said, "next week I'll be offering a special jumping clinic for any interested Horse Wise members. It will begin next Saturday and continue for a week, with intensive lessons all day on the weekends and after school on Tuesday and Thursday." He paused and looked around. "Now, are there any interested Horse Wise members here?"

Immediately hands shot up all around the ring.

Max smiled. "Great. You'll all be working hard, but you should be able to manage to have some fun, too."

"That's for sure," added Mrs. Reg. "Trust Max to leave out the best part. On the last day of the clinic, there will be a big party and dance here at Pine Hollow for all of the participants. You kids have all been working hard lately, and you'll be working even harder next week. We thought you deserved a celebration."

"Cool!" exclaimed Lorraine Olsen, one of Betsy's friends. "A dance sounds like fun!" She immediately began discussing the prospect with Betsy and Meg Durham.

"Another chance for those girls to act like idiots around the boys," Stevie commented sourly, watching them.

"Never mind them, Stevie," Carole said. "Aren't you excited about the jumping clinic? It will be a great chance to learn. You and Belle will have a chance to concentrate all your energy on jumping. It's really perfect timing for you, since you've been talking about doing more jumping with her." Belle was Stevie's horse. Stevie hadn't owned her for very long, so they were still learning a lot together. But Belle was a talented horse, and Stevie was a talented rider, and Carole was right. Max's jumping clinic couldn't have come at a better time for them.

"It's perfect timing for someone else, too," Lisa pointed out. "Merrill. Remember? I told you she's just started jumping. What an opportunity! She'll have a chance to learn from the best—Max."

Just then Joe Novick leaned over and joined their conversation. "I'll tell you what's good timing," he said with a grin. "That party on Saturday. It just happens to fall on my birthday."

"That's great," Stevie exclaimed. "Hey, Max, guess what? Joe's birthday is the day of the party!"

Max raised one eyebrow. "Really? Well, then, we'll have to think of something special to help Joe celebrate."

Joe waved one hand modestly. "Really, just a new car would be enough," he said.

Carole laughed. Noticing that Lisa wasn't laughing, she turned and saw that her friend had a funny look on her face. "What is it, Lisa?"

"I just remembered," Lisa said, a smile spreading over her face. "That same Saturday is Merrill's birthday, too! I had totally forgotten until Joe spoke up."

"Wow," Carole said. "Then the clinic and party will be like an extraspecial birthday treat for her—on top of visiting you, that is."

"That's right," Lisa said. "Being enrolled in Max's jumping clinic is the best birthday present any beginning jumper could have."

Just then Mrs. Reg, who had disappeared, returned with a bag.

"All right, everyone," Max said. "You all know how important it is to learn to bandage properly. Bandages protect your horse's delicate legs in all sorts of situations, including traveling in a trailer or van. Bandaging is a pretty basic skill, but one that always bears more practice. Today I'll be showing you a few tricks you can test out on your own legs. Then in a few minutes we'll try them out on the horses. Stevie, go ahead and pass out a bandage to each person."

Stevie nodded and dug into the bag. Pulling out a handful of neatly rolled and pinned bandages, she handed them out to Lorraine, Betsy, Adam, Meg, and Polly Giacomin.

"Hey, you forgot me, Stevie," said Veronica testily. She was sitting between Meg and Polly.

"Oh, sorry, Veronica," Stevie replied sweetly. She peered into the bag. "I think there's a very special bandage in here just for you, though." She reached in, pulled out a bandage, and handed it to Veronica.

Veronica stared down at the object in her hand. It looked just like the rest of the bandages except for one thing: Someone had written "Gucci" all over it.

As soon as the other students saw what Stevie had done, they burst out laughing. Veronica loved to brag about the expensive clothes she wore. She was a real snob when it came to designer labels, and everyone at Pine Hollow knew it. For her part, Stevie just stood back and grinned proudly.

Veronica stared at the bandage for a moment. Then she looked up at Stevie, with eyes narrowed. "I suppose this is your idea of a joke," she said coldly.

"As a matter of fact, it is," Stevie said, still grinning.

Veronica tossed her head. "Well, I think it's about time you grew up a little, Stevie Lake," she said. "These silly pranks might have been amusing when we were all children, but you can't keep acting like a five-year-old forever." With that, she tossed the Gucci bandage back into the bag Stevie was holding.

Stevie's grin faded. Without another word, she continued passing out the bandages.

"SHE HAS SOME NERVE," Stevie fumed to Carole and Lisa later. All three girls were busy wrapping and rewrapping the bandages as Max had showed them. "Who does she think she is, calling me a child in front of the whole class?"

"Don't take it so hard, Stevie," Lisa advised. "We all know Veronica is humor impaired."

"Right," Carole agreed. "That's why it's so much fun to play tricks on her, remember?"

"I guess so. But it still burns me up that she thinks she's so darned mature," Stevie said. "And Betsy Cavanaugh, too, for that matter. Just because she never thinks about anything but boys and dating and stuff doesn't make her any more mature than anybody else. I mean, I have a boyfriend too, for goodness' sake!" Stevie had been dating Phil Marsten, who lived in a town a few miles from Willow Creek, ever since they had met at summer riding camp.

Carole patted Stevie's arm. "We know."

Max sent a glance in their direction. "More wrapping and less talking, people," he said sternly.

The Saddle Club quieted down and concentrated on their bandages for the rest of the lesson.

"ANYBODY FOR A Saddle Club meeting at TD's?" asked Lisa, as the girls got ready to leave Pine Hollow later that day. TD's, also known as Tastee Delight, was an ice cream parlor at the local shopping center.

"Definitely," Stevie said. She dug into her pockets. "Oops, I guess I'm a little short of cash right now." She gave her friends a hopeful look.

"Sorry, Stevie," Carole said. "I'd lend you some money, but I barely have enough for myself today."

"Me too," Lisa said. "I spent most of my allowance on new film for my camera."

"Not to worry," Stevie said, glancing around. "Time for Plan B." She spotted Red O'Malley, Pine Hollow's stable hand, entering the locker room. "Make that Plan R."

She smiled at Red as he approached them. "Hello there, Red," she said. "How's it going?"

"Fine, Stevie," Red replied. "How are you?"

"Well, to tell you the truth, not too great," Stevie said sadly. "I just found out I have a very rare disease. It's a digestive thing."

"Really," Red commented drily. "How did you find out? Did Belle give you the diagnosis?"

"Of course not," Stevie replied disdainfully. "Don't be silly. Anyway, the problem is that I have to go on a very specific diet. I have to eat certain foods at certain times of the day or I'll waste away—"

"Let me guess," Red interrupted with a twinkle in his eyes. "Right now you're scheduled for ice cream, and you haven't got a cent."

Stevie gave a pathetic sigh. "You're so sensitive, Red. How did you know?"

"I guess I must have missed my calling to be a doctor," he said, digging into his pocket and pulling out a few dollars. "It's a good thing I didn't become a banker, though. This is the third time I've loaned you money this month, and I haven't seen a cent in return."

"Thanks a million, Red," Stevie said, taking the money from him. "I'll pay you back soon, really."

"Right," Red said, looking a little skeptical. "As soon as the story of your new ice-cream disease is made into a movie of the week, right?"

MOMENTS LATER THE girls slid into their favorite booth at TD's. The waitress came over to the table immediately. "Okay, let's get this over with," she said by way of greeting.

Stevie blinked up at the woman innocently. She knew very well that the reason for the waitress's comment was that Stevie always ordered outrageous ice cream concoctions, but she wasn't about to admit that. "I'm still making up my mind," she said sweetly. "Carole and Lisa, why don't you two go first?"

After Carole and Lisa had ordered, the waitress turned back to Stevie. "No more stalling," she said.

"Well, I'm in the mood for something a little different today," Stevie said. "So I think I'll have a scoop of mocha-hazelnut ice cream."

"That's it?" the waitress asked in disbelief.

"No, you interrupted me," Stevie said. "I'll also have a scoop of lime sherbet, with caramel topping and mini marshmallows." She leaned back, satisfied.

The waitress wrote it all down without another word. Then she spun on her heel and stalked away.

"Now," Stevie said to her friends, "it's time to talk about Merrill's visit. What fun things will we do while she's here?"

"I've been thinking about that," Lisa said. "I really want her to have a good time, especially since she'll be here for her birthday."

"How did you and Merrill meet, anyway?" Carole asked Lisa curiously. "I don't think you've ever told us."

"We met in a public speaking class our mothers made us take," Lisa explained. "My mother thought it would be a useful skill for me to learn."

"What a surprise," Stevie said with a laugh. Stevie and Carole knew that Lisa's mother liked to make her take all sorts of classes and lessons, from piano to tennis to ballet. She thought it would help turn Lisa into a proper young lady. It wasn't one of Lisa's favorite things about her mother, but at least one good thing had come of it: It had been Mrs. Atwood's idea for Lisa to take riding lessons.

"Anyway," Lisa continued, as the waitress appeared with their sundaes, "Merrill's mother made her take the course, too. Merrill's always been really quiet and shy, and her mother thought it would help her get over all that." She picked up her spoon and dug into her hot fudge sundae.

"Did it?" Carole asked.

Lisa shrugged. "Not really. For the last class, we each had to give a speech in front of our classmates and everybody's parents, and she was just terrified at the thought of getting up and talking in front of all those people. She worried about it more and more as the time to give the speeches got closer. Soon she couldn't think about anything else. She was even having trouble sleeping and eating because she was so nervous."

"Wow," Stevie said, trying to imagine that. She got nervous herself on occasion, but she never thought twice about giving a speech in class—unless she hadn't prepared for it, of course, which had been known to happen. In any case, she certainly couldn't imagine being so worried about speaking in front of people that she couldn't eat.

"What happened?" Carole asked. "Did she give the speech?"

Lisa nodded. "She begged her parents to let her drop out of the class, but they wouldn't let her. The night of the speeches, I found her in the bathroom. She was crying and shaking like a leaf. I knew I had to do something to help her." She shrugged. "I started off by reminding her of a trick our teacher told us: She could imagine that everyone in the audience was sitting there in their underwear."

Stevie grinned. "I've heard that one," she said.

"She didn't seem very convinced that that would work," Lisa continued. "So I said she could try picking out just a couple of people in the audience to focus on, so it would feel more like she was talking to one or two people rather than speaking in front of a crowd."

"That's a good idea," Carole said. "Did it work?"

"Well, not exactly," Lisa said. "She didn't seem very confident about that trick, either. So I figured it was time to get creative. I told her she should combine the two methods. She should go up there thinking that she could only look back and forth from me to our teacher, because everybody else was wearing pink polka-dot underwear. That did it. She actually started to smile. I just kept talking, describing all the weird and crazy underwear that everyone was wearing, and soon she was even laughing a little. By that time it was her turn to speak, so I got a seat in the front, and she gave her speech."

"How did it go?" Stevie asked.

"Okay," Lisa said. "She was still nervous, but she got through it. And I saw her smile when she looked around. We've been good friends ever since, even after her family moved to Maine."

Carole took a sip of her root-beer float. "I can't wait to meet her," she said. "I wonder if she's gotten any less timid since she started riding. Sometimes just being around horses can bring out the best in people."

"Like us, you mean?" Stevie queried with a smile.

"Exactly!" Carole replied, smiling back. "But seriously, look at what riding has done for all of us. It's made Lisa more independent; you more responsible, Stevie—"

"And you more organized?" Stevie added teasingly. Carole was definitely not organized—except when it came to horses.

Carole shrugged and laughed. "You got it."

Lisa looked thoughtful. "You know, you may be on to something, Carole. Horses just may be the key for Merrill, too. If she's a good rider, she'll be more self-confident."

"Right," Stevie agreed. "And this jumping clinic should help her become a better rider, and that will make her even more confident."

Lisa leaned back in her seat and sighed happily. "Now I really can't wait for her to get here," she said.

"Especially since there will be a big party for her on her birthday, thanks to Max," Carole pointed out.

"True," Stevie said, frowning a little. "I just hope the boy-crazy girls don't ruin it for the rest of us."

"What makes you think they will?" Carole asked.

Stevie shrugged. "You know how they are. They'll try to make anything into a big mushy romantic event."

"That could be kind of a challenge. There aren't that many boys in our class," Lisa pointed out.

"True," Stevie said, looking thoughtful. "But that gives me a great idea."

Carole and Lisa exchanged a nervous glance. Stevie's great ideas had a tendency to land her, and often her friends, in hot water.

Stevie noticed the glance. "Don't worry," she said quickly.

"All I was thinking was that I should ask Max if I can invite Phil to the party, and maybe A.J., too. That way those girls will see that there are at least a couple of boys who are too sensible to be affected by their giggles and flirting." A.J. was Phil's best friend. The Saddle Club liked him a lot—he was funny and down-to-earth, just like Phil.

"Great," Carole said. "It would be fun to have them there anyway, no matter what Betsy and the others think of it."

"Good. I'll ask Max tomorrow." Stevie squirmed happily in her seat. "We have so many things to look forward to. I can hardly wait for next Friday. There's just one problem."

"What's that?" asked Lisa.

Stevie sighed. "It seems like a million years away!"

DESPITE STEVIE'S FEARS, the next Friday arrived right on schedule. Stevie and Carole met at Pine Hollow after school to do a few chores and to wait for Lisa and Merrill, who were coming straight from the airport.

"Did you talk to Phil yet?" Carole asked as the two girls sorted grain in the feed shed.

"Uh-huh," Stevie said. "He's coming. A.J. too."

"Great," Carole said. She glanced at her watch and stood up. "Come on, we're finished, and Lisa and Merrill should be here any minute."

The two friends left the shed and headed into the stable. They didn't have long to wait before they heard the sound of a car pulling up in front of the stable. Hurrying outside, they saw Lisa climbing out of her mother's car, followed by a slim, pretty girl with long strawberry-blond hair.

"Hi, guys," Lisa called to her friends. "Come and meet Merrill."

"It's nice to meet both of you," Merrill said shyly. "Lisa has told me a lot about you."

"Same here," Stevie said.

"She told us you're becoming a good rider," Carole said.

Lisa laughed. "Didn't I tell you Carole always thinks about horses first?" she said to Merrill.

"And second, and third," Stevie added. "It's just one of her charms."

Merrill smiled. "That's okay," she said, brushing her hair away from her face. "I like talking about horses, too."

"That's good enough for me," Carole declared. "I feel like we're friends already."

"Now let's meet some other friends," Lisa suggested.

"You mean like Prancer and Starlight and Belle?" Carole guessed. Starlight was Carole's horse, and Prancer was the pretty Thoroughbred mare Lisa usually rode.

Lisa nodded and led the way into the stable. Before long Merrill had been introduced to every horse in the place. The more Stevie and Carole talked to her, the more they liked her. Behind her shyness she was very smart and funny, and it was obvious that she loved horses as much as The Saddle Club did. After they had greeted the horses, the girls went to look for Max to ask his permission to go on a quick trail ride.

"I just hope the horses here aren't too much for me," Merrill commented worriedly. "The stable where I ride is much smaller than this. I haven't ridden that many different horses since I started."

"I'm sure you'll do fine," Carole assured her. "Max's horses are very well trained."

They found Max in Mrs. Reg's office.

"Hi, Max," Lisa said. "This is Merrill—she's the one I told you about who'll be taking your jumping clinic with us."

"Hello, Merrill," Max said. "I'm glad to meet you. So you've been taking lessons up in Maine?"

Merrill nodded. "I've been riding for only a few months," she said softly. "I hope I'll be able to keep up in your classes. I haven't really jumped very much at all."

"No problem," Max said. "We've got all levels of riders participating. It will be a terrific chance for you to learn."

"Can we take Merrill for a trail ride?" Carole asked.

"Sure thing," Max said. "Which horse do you think she should ride?"

Carole thought for a moment. Merrill seemed a little nervous about riding a strange horse, and she wanted to pick one that would help her relax. "How about Patch?" she suggested. Patch was good with beginning riders.

Max nodded. "Good choice. Just make sure you're back before dark."

The girls headed for the student locker room to change into riding clothes. The young riders at Pine Hollow each had a cubbyhole where he or she kept boots, clothing, and other equipment. Today, when Stevie reached into hers, she felt something very strange—and sticky. She pulled out her hand and stared at it. "Yuck," she said.

Carole looked over and wrinkled her nose. "What's that?" she asked.

Stevie touched her tongue to one finger. "Just as I thought," she said grimly. "Sugar."

"How did you get sugar in your cubby?" Lisa asked.

"*I* didn't," Stevie said. "But someone did." She emptied the cubby. Everything was covered in a layer of sticky crystals. Apparently, someone had dumped a whole box of sugar over the cubby's contents and then added enough water to turn it into a sticky, congealed mess.

"Who would do something like that?" Merrill asked.

Stevie, Carole, and Lisa exchanged looks and replied in one voice, "Veronica."

"This must be her subtle way of getting back at you for that Gucci bandage last week," Carole guessed. She explained the trick Stevie had played on Veronica.

"Sounds like she can't take a joke," Merrill said.

"That's for sure," Stevie said angrily. "She's not much good at playing them, either. Just look at this mess!" She gestured to her sugar-coated clothes. "It will take me hours to get it all clean. At least *my* joke was funny." She leaned over and picked up her sugar-encrusted hairbrush between two fingers. "This isn't funny at all. It's just plain mean."

Lisa shook her head. "So much for Veronica being mature," she said. "Are you going to tell Max?"

"I don't think so," Stevie said. "Although it's tempting because he might kick her out of Horse Wise for good. But I don't have any proof that she did it, and besides . . ."

"Besides what?" Carole prompted.

Stevie tossed her head. "Besides, I'd rather get back at her myself."

A FEW MINUTES later the girls were riding out across the fields and meadows behind Pine Hollow. Stevie had borrowed Carole's spare boots, since her own were full of sugar.

Merrill was doing very well so far on Patch. Carole suspected that Merrill would be fine on a more spirited horse—she held the reins lightly, maintaining good contact with Patch's mouth, and Patch was responding well to all of her aids. Still, Carole was glad she'd suggested starting her out on Patch. Since Merrill was new to jumping, it would help her to ride a reliable horse. And this trail ride would give her a chance to get to know him before the first clinic class the next day.

"Tell us about your stable in Maine," Carole said to Merrill as the four girls rode side by side across a wide field.

"Well, it's pretty small, like I said," Merrill said. "A woman named Mary Bartlett owns it and teaches all the classes. She has about a dozen horses and ponies."

"Do you like her?" Stevie asked.

Merrill nodded. "A lot. She's really patient with all the students. You can tell the horses love her, too. She's great with all kinds of animals."

"Tell them about Maine," Lisa suggested. "It always sounds so beautiful the way you describe it in your letters."

"It is," Merrill said. "I live in a coastal town called Ellsworth, not far from Mount Desert Island, where Acadia National Park is located. So there's lots of really pretty scenery, especially around Mary's stable." She looked around and took a deep breath of the crisp Virginia air. "Of course, the land around here is pretty gorgeous, too."

"Especially from horseback," Carole agreed.

"You think anyplace looks gorgeous from horseback, Carole," Stevie pointed out.

Carole shrugged. "It does," she said.

The others couldn't argue with that. They rode in silence for a few minutes. Finally Merrill spoke up.

"I'm a little nervous about the jumping clinic," she said, "but I'm kind of excited, too."

"There's nothing like it," Lisa said. "You'll love it."

"I think I will," Merrill said dreamily. "Sailing over everything in your path, over hill and dale, just like flying."

"Well, it's not quite as easy as that," Carole cautioned. "You have to learn the proper form, and how to position your horse and help him adjust his stride . . ."

Stevie rolled her eyes. "Yeah, yeah," she said. "But even with all that stuff, it still does feel kind of like you're flying."

"I guess you're right," Carole said. She smiled at Merrill. "I'm sure you'll do great."

"I hope so," Merrill said. "Especially since . . ."

"Especially since what?" Lisa prompted.

"Well, I haven't even told you this yet, Lisa," Merrill said. "But my parents just told me that if I want one, they'll buy me my own horse for my birthday."

Carole gasped. "*If* you want one? That's wonderful!"

"It sure is," Lisa said. "You must be so excited!"

"I am," Merrill admitted. "But I don't want to choose the wrong horse."

"I don't blame you," Stevie said. "Having the right horse is important." She reached forward and gave Belle a fond pat on the neck.

"How did you know Belle was the right horse for you?" Merrill asked.

Stevie shrugged. "I just knew as soon as I rode her that I liked her. And the more I rode her, the more I knew she was the horse for me. Soon I could hardly imagine *not* riding her."

"That's exactly how it was with Starlight," Carole said.

Merrill sighed. "It sounds wonderful," she said. "I hope I can find a horse as special as the ones you guys have."

"You will," Carole assured her. She smiled. "What a way to celebrate your birthday—finding your very own horse."

"Speaking of celebrating," Stevie said, "we still have to decide how we're going to help Merrill celebrate next weekend."

Merrill blushed. "Oh, you don't have to do anything—"

Stevie cut her off with a wave of her hand. "Don't be silly," she declared. "Of course we have to do something special. Something fun. You heard about the big party on Saturday, didn't you?"

Merrill looked nervous. "Big party? What do you mean?"

"Max is having a dance to celebrate at the end of the clinic," Lisa explained. "I guess I forgot to tell you."

"One of the other riders at Pine Hollow has his birthday on Saturday," Carole said, "so we are going to make it sort of a birthday party for both of you."

"I don't want you to make a big fuss or anything," Merrill said quietly. "I don't really like being the center of attention."

"Don't worry about a thing," Stevie said. She couldn't understand how anybody couldn't like being the center of attention at a party. Stevie herself loved it. And she was sure that Merrill would love it, too, if she gave it a chance. "We won't embarrass you." She gave the visitor a devilish wink and a grin. "Not *too* much, anyway."

Merrill still looked a little worried, but she smiled back.

4

"Is everybody ready to do some serious jumping?" Stevie asked the next morning, sitting down beside her friends in the indoor ring, where Max had told them to gather.

"I know I am," Carole declared. Carole hadn't thought about much else for the past week. The night before she had reread the sections on jumping in several of her riding books. She couldn't wait to get started.

"How many people are in this class?" Merrill asked, glancing around at the other riders.

"Max said there will be twelve, including us," Lisa replied. She looked around, too. "It looks like almost everyone is here already."

"Including everyone's favorite person," Stevie added, nodding toward the door as Veronica strolled in.

"Is that the girl you think put sugar in your cubby?" Merrill asked.

"No, that's the girl I *know* put sugar in my cubby," Stevie said. "And she's going to pay for it, too—mark my words."

Just then Veronica turned and noticed Merrill. She wandered over. "So who's the new girl?" she asked, smiling.

Merrill smiled back. "I'm Merrill Minot," she said. "I'm visiting Lisa, and Max is letting me be in the jumping clinic."

Veronica carefully took in Merrill's neat, stylish outfit and long, shining hair and seemed to like what she saw. "Well, welcome to Pine Hollow," she said. "If you have any questions about anything, just ask me."

"Thanks," Merrill said, as The Saddle Club exchanged surprised glances. They couldn't believe it: Merrill had passed Veronica's inspection even though she was their friend.

"Hi there," said Joe Novick, coming over to join them.

"Hi, Joe!" Veronica said with a big smile. "How are you?"

"Fine, thanks," he replied. Then he turned to Merrill. "You're Lisa's friend Merrill, right? I hear we have the same birthday," he said.

Merrill blushed. "I guess so. I mean, they told me someone else's birthday was the same as mine. I mean, um, yes."

Joe didn't seem to notice Merrill's nervousness. He smiled down at her. "By the way, my name's Joe."

"Oh, um, hi," Merrill said, still blushing.

Veronica tossed her hair, obviously annoyed that Joe was ignoring her. "So, Joe," she said sweetly. "Do you have anything special planned for your birthday?"

Joe shrugged. "Just the clinic and then Max's party."

"You mean Max's *dance*," Veronica corrected.

"Whatever," Joe said. He glanced over toward the door as Max entered. "It looks like it's time to get started." He smiled again at Merrill. "I'm sure I'll see you later."

She nodded mutely. He loped away, with Veronica right behind him.

"I think he likes you, Merrill," Lisa said.

Merrill shrugged. "I don't think so," she said. "I sounded like an idiot talking to him."

"Don't be silly," Stevie said authoritatively. "Boys never notice that kind of thing."

"Do you speak from experience?" Carole teased.

Stevie stuck out her tongue, but she didn't have time to reply. It was time for class to begin.

"All right, everyone," Max said, stepping in front of the group. "First of all, we're going to start by talking a little bit about why we all want to learn to jump."

"So we can fly, right?" Lisa whispered to Merrill. Merrill smiled and nodded.

Max went on to talk about the various horse show classes, such as hunter and open jumper, as well as foxhunting, steeplechasing, and other equestrian sports.

"So you see," he finished, "there are lots of reasons to learn to jump, and if you're going to learn, you should learn well. That applies to both the rider and the horse. I like to think that all of my horses have been exceptionally trained—or are in that process now." He shot a glance toward Lisa. She knew he was referring to Prancer. The mare had originally been trained as a racehorse, so jumping was still fairly new to her.

"Since the focus of this clinic is on helping you become better riders more than helping the horses become better jumpers—although of course that never hurts—we'll be using more experienced horses for these classes."

Carole reached over and gave Lisa's arm a sympathetic squeeze. Lisa's friends knew that Max had already discussed this with Lisa. Because Prancer was still so green, he wanted Lisa to ride Barq, one of the older horses, during the clinic. Carole and Stevie knew that Lisa was a little disappointed—she loved riding the young Thoroughbred. But they also knew that Max was right. Lisa would have an easier time learning aboard the steadier, more experienced Barq. And whatever she learned could only help her when she went back to riding Prancer.

Max assigned a horse to each rider. Stevie and Carole were on their own horses, as were Veronica, who owned a gorgeous new Thoroughbred named Danny, and Polly Giacomin, who owned a frisky brown gelding named Romeo. "Lisa, you'll be riding Barq," Max said, glancing down at his list. "Merrill Minot will ride Patch. Meg Durham has Comanche, Betsy Cavanaugh will take Topside, Adam Levine is on Delilah. Simon Atherton, you will ride Bluegrass; Joe Novick will ride Rusty; and Lorraine Olsen, you're on Diablo. Everybody got it?"

Everybody did. It was time to tack up.

"You'll do fine on Barq, Lisa," Carole told her friend as they walked toward their horses' stalls. "He's a good, steady jumper."

"I know," Lisa said. "I really don't mind not riding Prancer for the clinic—it wouldn't be fair to ask that much of her when it's all still so new to her."

Carole nodded and smiled. She should have known that Lisa's sensible nature would make her see the best side of the situation. They parted in front of Starlight's stall.

Fifteen minutes later the students were mounted in the outdoor ring. Max had set up some cavalletti—long, thin poles that could be set on the ground or at various low heights, which were often used in training horses to jump. After the students practiced proper jumping position on the flat for a while, Max set them to work over the cavalletti.

Lisa finished one of her turns. She glanced over at Merrill, who was about to start her round. Merrill's face was glowing, and while she was obviously concentrating hard on what she was doing, she seemed to be enjoying herself, too. Lisa was glad of that. Even though Merrill was the least experienced rider in the class except for Simon, she was holding her own with the other students.

Finally Max called for a lunch break. The students trooped inside to the locker room for sandwiches and sodas. The Saddle Club and Merrill sat down together in a corner of the room and started talking about the morning's work.

"You were right about Max," Merrill said, taking a big bite of her ham sandwich. "He's a great teacher."

"That's true," Carole said. "But you're a pretty good student, too, especially since you've hardly jumped before."

Merrill shrugged and looked down at her hands. "Well, I'm trying, but I know I'm doing a lot of things wrong. I always forget to keep my arms loose, and during that last round my legs were wobbling all over the place."

"Everybody makes those mistakes when they're first learning," Stevie said. "You heard how Max kept yelling about my hand position. And I've been jumping for years."

"There's so much to remember," Merrill said.

Lisa nodded. "It's true. But when you've learned everything really well and had enough practice, and when you're confident, it all comes together and you get that magical flying feeling we were talking about."

Merrill smiled. "I can't wait," she said.

AFTER LUNCH THE group returned to the outdoor ring. Max and Red had set up a few low jumps.

Once the horses were warmed up again, Max had the riders line up while he told them a little bit about the course he had laid out. "Now we're going to move on to something a little more challenging," he said. "Of course you all know that the approach to the jump is more important than anything that comes after. In this case, you should take your horse into a steady trot for the approach to the first fence. After landing, you should need about ten cantering strides before the second fence, then six strides to the third. Any questions?"

Polly Giacomin raised her hand. "Won't we have to make some adjustments according to the length of our horses' strides?"

"You might," Max said. "That's when it's important to remember that you can control the length of your mount's stride. Extension and collection, remember?"

"I hope I'm ready for this," Merrill whispered to Carole. "There's so much to know."

"You'll do fine," Carole whispered back. "It is hard when everything is so new, but just remember: Patch is a pro, even if you aren't."

Merrill smiled gratefully. "I'm glad of that," she said, giving the pinto gelding a pat.

Soon Max finished talking, and it was time for the students to try the course. Carole went first.

"Nice work, Carole," Max said when she had finished. "Your form was almost perfect. The only thing I noticed was that you looked off to one side between the second and third fences, and that made Starlight waver for a second."

Carole apologized. "A crow landed on the fence, and then I saw it in the corner of my eye."

Max nodded, glancing at the large black bird, still perched on the fence. "Well, at least you and Starlight recovered well. It didn't affect your last jump at all." He turned to the rest of the class. "That's an important thing to remember, not just in jumping, but in all riding. If something unexpected happens, a good rider must adjust and work through it. That's what Carole did. She made a mistake, but instead of letting that throw off her whole performance, she corrected herself. But let's also remember that your head is fairly heavy. When you turn it, your horse feels that."

"I didn't even know Carole made a mistake," Merrill said quietly to Lisa, her eyes wide. "I'm not sure I'm ready for this."

"Don't worry," Lisa said. "Simon's going next, and he's not as good a rider as you are."

The class watched as Simon Atherton bumbled his way over the obstacles. His horse, Bluegrass, was a very steady and obedient mount, but Simon's flopping arms and legs and his awkward riding posture threw off the horse's stride. Bluegrass refused the first fence, and stopped and stepped over the second one instead of jumping it. Simon managed to get him to jump the third fence, but as soon as he was over, Bluegrass stopped short and refused to move for several seconds. Finally, the flustered Simon managed to bring his horse back into line with the others.

Max shot a stern look at Meg and Betsy, who were giggling at Simon's performance. They quieted down immediately. Then Max explained to Simon what had gone wrong. But he did it in a constructive way, so he sounded less critical of Simon's major mistakes than he had been of Carole's relatively minor error. Carole knew that that was what made Max a good instructor—he could be stern and strict, but he also knew when to encourage and comfort his students.

Veronica diAngelo went next, and she jumped the course very well. She was a better-than-average rider when she put her mind to it, and her horse was extremely talented and well trained. Max gave her a few pointers and then nodded to Joe Novick, who was next. But as Veronica returned to her place, she brought Danny a little too close to Meg's horse, Comanche, who snorted in annoyance and kicked out. Comanche didn't hit Danny, but the big Thoroughbred shied to one side, bumping into Patch, who threw up his head and danced sideways nervously.

"Don't drop your reins," Carole called to Merrill anxiously. "Don't let Patch forget you're in charge."

Merrill had been taken by surprise, but she tried to do as Carole said. Luckily Patch was too even-tempered to act up any more, but Carole thought he still seemed a little skittish. She hoped he would calm down soon.

Joe and the next few riders did fairly well over the course. Most of them had been jumping for some time, and the course wasn't very challenging. Max watched them all carefully and instructed them on ways to improve their jumping positions to make their rides cleaner.

When Max nodded to Merrill, she nodded back grimly. Carole, Stevie, and Lisa could see that neither she nor Patch had quite recovered from the scare Danny had given them. But Merrill quickly urged her horse into a trot and sent him toward the first obstacle. Patch shook his head, annoyed by the overly tight hold Merrill had on the reins. He pranced sideways a little on the approach, but made it over the first fence. Merrill gave him a little more freedom with the reins. Patch settled down and went over the next two fences without trouble, though his form wasn't as controlled as it should have been.

White-faced, Merrill brought him to a stop in front of Max. Her hands were shaking as they held the reins. It was obvious to everyone that she hadn't had an easy time.

"All right, Merrill. You finished," Max began. "But there's one important thing you should have done at the start. Your horse was nervous; he could have used a half turn around the ring to calm him down. Instead, you made him begin right away."

Merrill nodded mutely.

"But don't be discouraged," Max said gently. "You did some good things, too, like correcting your hand position after the first jump. And your seat was quite good." He turned back to the group. "All right, Betsy, you're next."

Merrill rode back to her place beside Carole. "I was terrible, wasn't I?" she moaned. "I'm so embarrassed."

"Don't be," Carole told her. "You heard what Max said. You did a lot of things right."

"I did more things wrong," Merrill said. "I'm the worst rider here. I shouldn't even be in this class. It's obvious I'm not ready to start jumping."

"That's ridiculous," Carole said firmly. "Just remember, the important thing is to learn from your mistakes and try to correct them the next time around. That's what this clinic is all about, for all of us. And like Max said earlier, you've got to be able to recover from a mistake, or from a bad round, or even from a bad day. Everybody has them."

Merrill nodded but didn't reply. Carole just hoped her words had made sense to the other girl.

After everyone's turn, Max spoke about some of the more common errors people were making and how to correct them. "Now, with those things in mind, let's all try it again," he said. "Carole, go ahead."

Most of the students learned from their first attempt. Carole completed an almost flawless ride, as did Veronica and Stevie. Even Simon seemed a little more confident.

Then it was Merrill's turn again. She glanced at Carole and gulped, but she looked a little calmer than she had at the beginning. Carole hoped that meant Merrill was feeling more confident. She crossed her fingers just in case.

Merrill rode forward and took Patch in a circle at a brisk trot before aiming him for the first fence. She was sitting well, her hands steady and light on the reins. Patch seemed relaxed but alert. His ears pricked forward, and his trot was even as he got closer to the low fence.

Then it happened.

With a loud caw, the crow, which had been perched on the fence of the ring watching the people and horses, launched itself into the air and circled above the riders.

Patch, who had just reached the first fence, was startled by the sudden noise and motion. Instead of jumping up and forward, he wheeled around and shied sideways, crashing into the fence. Scared even more by the impact, he reared up and twisted around, ending up straddling the remains of the jump. Merrill had barely managed to keep her seat and was clinging to Patch's mane, her stirrups swinging free of her feet. Max was already hurrying forward to catch the panicky horse, but Patch was too quick for him. He reared again, unseating Merrill completely, and then darted away as the girl tumbled off and landed hard on her backside.

Lisa slid out of the saddle and tossed Barq's reins to Carole. She ran to Merrill's side.

"Are you okay?" she asked anxiously.

Merrill shook her head, tears running down her face. "I think I'm okay," she said in a shaky voice.

"Hey, are you all right, Merrill?" Joe Novick asked, joining them. There was a look of real concern on his face. "That was quite a tumble."

Merrill quickly wiped her face with the back of her hand, which only succeeded in leaving a trail of dirt mixed with the tears on her face. "Um . . . ," she said.

"Here." Joe reached into the pocket of his jeans and pulled out a crumpled but clean tissue. Lisa took it from him and wiped off Merrill's face. Then she and Joe helped Merrill stand.

"I don't think anything's broken," Merrill said. She reached behind her gingerly. "Only bruised."

By this time Max had caught and calmed Patch. The gelding looked a little ashamed of himself.

"Tough break, Merrill," Max said. "Are you in one piece?"

Merrill nodded. "I think so."

"Patch is pretty calm most of the time, but he has a tendency to shy at loud noises," Max explained, patting the horse on the neck.

"I know," Lisa added, her eyes widening as she remembered her very first ride at Pine Hollow. She, too, had been riding Patch when there had been a loud, sudden noise. That time it had been Veronica slamming a door, and it had made Patch take off and jump out of the ring. Lisa hadn't fallen off, but the incident had scared her.

Still, it was clear that this fall had scared Merrill even more. And that worried Lisa. She was sure that Merrill would have quit the public speaking course if her parents had let her. And she knew that Merrill had once dropped out of a gymnastics class after taking a fall off the balance beam. Now that she'd fallen off, would Merrill want to stop riding altogether?

Max helped Merrill climb back into Patch's saddle. Merrill looked anxious, but once she was aboard she seemed to regain control. She took Patch around the ring at a walk and then at a trot. As if trying to make up for his bad behavior, Patch behaved perfectly.

"Do you want to try that fence again, Merrill?" Max asked. "It might be good for Patch—and for you."

"Could I wait for my next turn?" Merrill said. "I think I need a few minutes."

Max nodded understandingly. "Okay, who's next?" he asked, seeming satisfied that everything was all right.

But when Merrill took her place in line again, Carole could see that she still looked scared. "Are you okay?" she whispered. "Really?"

When Merrill looked at her, Carole saw tears glistening in the other girl's eyes. But Merrill kept them under control. "I'm fine," she replied. "I just hope I don't have to take another turn jumping today."

Carole glanced at her watch. "It's getting pretty late," she said. "I bet this will be the last round. Max won't want to overtire the horses—or us."

She was right. After the last rider had finished the course for the second time, Max announced that it was time to take the horses in. "We had a good class today, everyone," he added. "More to come tomorrow—don't be late."

* * *

A LITTLE LATER, The Saddle Club and Merrill sat together cleaning their tack and talking about the day. Foremost in all their minds was Merrill's fall.

"Everyone has a ride like that once in a while," Carole told her again, soaping up Starlight's saddle. "You just have to learn to get past it and remember it's all part of the learning process."

"I know," Merrill said. "It's just that I'm not sure anymore how much I want to learn."

"What do you mean?" Lisa asked, her stomach sinking. "You don't want to give up riding, do you?"

Merrill shook her head. "No, I definitely don't want to give up riding. I love it too much."

"Well, that's settled," Stevie said. "Tomorrow is another day. You'll make up for today then, and before long you'll be jumping like a pro."

"I'm not so sure about that," Merrill said quietly.

"Okay, maybe it will take a little longer than that before you're really a pro," Stevie corrected herself. "But it will happen, trust me."

"It might not happen for me," Merrill said, "because I'm not sure I want to learn to jump anymore."

Lisa gasped. "Not learn to jump? But why? Because a bird scared your horse today?"

"It's not that," Merrill said, biting her lip. "There's just so much to remember. It seems a lot harder than other kinds of riding. I'm not sure it's worth it to me."

The Saddle Club exchanged a worried glance. They couldn't let Merrill give up on jumping!

"What about what you were saying earlier?" Lisa said. "About jumping being sort of like flying. You wouldn't want to miss out on that, would you?"

Merrill shrugged. "Maybe." But she looked doubtful.

Stevie seized the opportunity. "I for one don't think you should let one day's experience decide something that important," she said. "You've got to give it at least one more chance. Otherwise you'll always wonder whether you made the right choice."

"Stevie's right," Carole urged Merrill. "Try it again tomorrow and see how it goes. Please?"

Merrill looked uncertain. "Well . . . ," she said. "I really didn't feel very comfortable even before I fell."

An idea occurred to Carole. "Maybe you need to try a different horse," she suggested. "Maybe you and Patch just didn't click. Anyway, it's always a good idea for a rider to try out different kinds of horses. I'm sure Max would let you switch." Carole really didn't think incompatibility with Patch was the problem. But maybe it would make Merrill feel better to ride a different horse. Desperate times called for desperate measures.

"Do you think he would?" Merrill asked slowly. She thought for a moment. "Well, maybe I should give it one more try—"

"Great!" Stevie interrupted before the other girl could change her mind. She jumped to her feet. "I'll go ask Max right now!" She hurried out of the room.

5

THE NEXT MORNING Carole, Stevie, and Lisa arrived at Pine Hollow an hour before the jumping clinic. Merrill was spending the morning with an elderly aunt who lived nearby, and The Saddle Club had decided to take advantage of her absence by having a secret birthday-planning meeting. Of course, since the meeting was taking place at Pine Hollow, that meant the girls had to work while they talked. There was nothing Max and Mrs. Reg hated seeing more than a pair of idle hands—except maybe *three* pairs of idle hands. So the girls settled down in the tack room with a pile of stirrups and bits that needed polishing.

"Okay," Stevie said as they all set to work. "The first order of business is coming up with something fun and exciting to do for Merrill on her birthday."

"Not *too* exciting, though," Lisa cautioned. "Remember, Stevie, Merrill doesn't quite have your taste for, uh, adventure. We don't want to embarrass her."

"Also, don't forget that Saturday is Joe Novick's birthday, too," Carole said. "If we do something special for Merrill, we should include him."

"Especially since it's obvious to everyone except Merrill that he really likes her," Lisa added.

Stevie smirked. "It was pretty obvious to Veronica, that's for sure. And it's pretty obvious she doesn't like it. You should have seen her face when Joe jumped down and ran to Merrill's rescue after she fell yesterday."

"I know," Carole said. "And she walked by yesterday when they were talking together after we finished cleaning tack. If looks could kill, Merrill would be a goner. I guess Veronica thought that after Betsy ditched Joe, he would be hers for the picking."

"Luckily I don't think Merrill even saw Veronica walk by," Lisa said.

"No kidding," Stevie said. "She was too busy gazing at Joe to notice anybody else."

Lisa laughed. "She may be shy, but she seems to be getting over it a little with Joe, at least. The crazy thing is, she still insists she has no interest in him—and, of course, she also insists that there's no way he could ever have any interest in her."

"Oh, he's interested all right," Stevie declared. "And so is she. That could be a very good thing. Joe is in the clinic—one more reason for her not to drop out."

Lisa shook her head. "I don't think so," she said. "Merrill isn't like that. She's never been boy-crazy, and she can be pretty stubborn. Once she makes up her mind about something, nothing will change it."

"In that case, I think we should make keeping Merrill in the clinic an official Saddle Club project," Stevie said.

"That's a great idea," Lisa exclaimed. "If anybody can help Merrill through her jumping problems, it's us. Carole started by suggesting that Merrill try a different horse today."

Carole nodded. "I hope it helps her. As with most riding problems, Merrill's is really all in her head."

"Okay, now that that's settled, let's get down to some serious party planning," Stevie said, tossing a polished snaffle bit into the trunk by her feet. "What can we do to turn Max's party into a birthday bash for Merrill and Joe?"

"Well, we should have a cake for starters," Carole said.

"That goes without saying," Stevie said. "Who wants to be in charge of that?"

"I will," Lisa volunteered. "I'm sure my mother will want to make it."

"Good. Now what else?" Stevie asked. She thought hard for a minute. "I know. We could ask everyone to bring some kind of funny gag gift for Merrill, and make her open them in front of everyone."

Lisa looked dubious. "I don't think she'd like that," she said. "Remember what she said about being the center of attention? Well, I'd say that definitely qualifies."

"Besides, everyone would have to bring something for Joe, too," Carole said, "and that could get expensive."

"Well, how about if we make Merrill and Joe wear some kind of special birthday costume—maybe a big hat or something," Stevie said. "Or have a dance contest and make them be the judges. Or both!"

Carole shook her head. "All of these things would be great ideas if it were *your* birthday. But they don't seem like anything Merrill would enjoy at all."

"You're right," Lisa said. "And we definitely don't want to make her miserable. We have to think of something that won't make her feel embarrassed."

The three girls thought in silence. Nothing any of them could come up with seemed quite right.

Finally Carole glanced at her watch. "We're not getting anywhere," she commented. "What time is Merrill getting here?"

"I'm not sure," Lisa said. "She said she would definitely be in time for the clinic, but she wasn't sure of the exact time. I think she went with her aunt to some early-morning swap meet at her church."

Suddenly Stevie straightened up in her seat. "That's it!" she cried.

"What?" Carole and Lisa asked in one voice.

"I have the perfect idea for Saturday," Stevie said. "The swap meet just made me think of it. We'll have a Yankee Swap!"

Lisa smiled. "That's perfect!" she exclaimed.

Carole looked confused. "A Yankee what?"

"Swap," Stevie said. "It's a fun way to exchange gifts. See, each person who'll be at the party draws the name of another guest out of a hat. Everyone buys and wraps a gift for the person whose name he or she got."

"Like a Secret Santa exchange," Carole said with a shrug.

"But wait, there's more," Lisa said.

"Right," Stevie continued. "At the party, all the gifts go in one big pile. None of them have name tags, so no one knows which gift is meant for who. Or is it 'whom'? Anyway, someone is chosen to start, and that person picks a gift from the pile and opens it. The next person picks a gift, too. But the thing is, that person can decide either to keep the gift they got *or* exchange it with the first person's."

"It goes that way all down the line," Lisa explained. "The third person can keep the gift she gets or trade—I mean *swap*—with either of the people who went before. And so on."

Carole nodded. "I think I get it," she said. "I guess the fun part is seeing who ends up with the gifts that were actually intended for them after all that swapping, right?"

"Right," Stevie confirmed. "It can really be a lot of fun."

"Let's do it!" Lisa declared. "It's completely perfect. It lets us celebrate Merrill's birthday *and* Joe's, without really putting either of them in the spotlight."

Stevie laughed. "Joe might be a little disappointed by that," she said. "He *likes* being in the spotlight."

"He'll get over it," Carole replied. "And anyway, we'll still have the cake for them. But this way, since Merrill will know about the swap ahead of time, she won't be embarrassed by any major surprises."

Lisa's expression sobered. "I just hope Merrill makes it through the clinic so she'll be at the party," she said.

"Don't worry," Carole said reassuringly. "She will. The Saddle Club is going to make sure of that, remember?"

MERRILL ARRIVED AT the stable a short time later. The Saddle Club quickly filled her in on their plan.

"A Yankee Swap?" Merrill repeated. "Why do they call it that?"

Stevie shrugged. "I never thought about it," she said. "But now that you mention it, I guess it's even more appropriate. A Yankee is someone from up north, right? And that's where you're from now."

"Isn't it sometimes used in a derogatory way, though?" Lisa commented.

"Translation please," Stevie said. "What does 'derogatory' mean?"

"It means negative, or something like that," Lisa explained. "I've heard the word 'Yankee' used as a put-down."

"Well, if that's the case, I like Stevie's definition better," Carole said. "No matter how some people may use it, I think saying someone's a Yankee can just be a way of describing where they live."

"And if you're using it that way, it's fine with me," Merrill said. "I love Maine, so I don't mind if someone calls me a Yankee."

"Good," Stevie said. "That's settled. So the Yankee Swap is on, right?"

Merrill hesitated. "I'm still not sure about having a birthday party with a bunch of kids I hardly know," she said.

"Don't worry," Stevie replied. "The others will barely even notice the Swap is for you, because this way everyone gets a present. It's more like a birthday party for everyone."

"Well . . . when you put it that way, it does kind of sound like fun," Merrill said. She smiled tentatively. "Count me in, I guess."

"COME ON, IT'S almost time for class to start," Carole said a few minutes later. "Max said Merrill could ride a different horse today. Let's go ask him which one is available."

"While we're at it, we can tell him our idea for the Yankee Swap," Stevie added. "I'm sure he'll love it."

The four girls found Max in the hallway. "Hello, girls," he greeted them. "All ready for the clinic today?"

"That's what we wanted to talk to you about," Stevie said. "You said that Merrill could try a different horse today, remember?"

Max nodded and looked at Merrill. "Didn't you like Patch, Merrill?"

Merrill shrugged, not meeting his eye. "I don't think we hit it off that well. You saw how much trouble I was having yesterday."

"And do you think that was because of Patch?" Max asked.

"Well, no . . ." Merrill's face turned red.

Carole could see that the other girl was becoming flustered, so she stepped forward. "It was actually my idea that she try a different horse, Max," she said. "Merrill had such a bad day yesterday that I thought it might help if she had a fresh start. It's not that she's blaming Patch for anything, but we just thought a different horse might give her a different perspective on things." The explanation sounded a little weak even to Carole, but Max looked thoughtful.

"All right, then," Max said. "Why don't you try Chippewa today, Merrill. He's not being used by anyone else in the class, and he's a good steady jumper. These girls can show you to his stall."

"Thanks, Max," Lisa said gratefully.

"But wait," Stevie said as Max started to turn away. "We have one more question for you. It has to do with the party on Saturday." She outlined the plan for the Yankee Swap.

By the time she finished, Max was smiling. "That sounds like a great plan," he said. "On one condition."

"What's that?" Stevie asked.

"The condition is that Red, Mother, and I get to be a part of it," Max said, his eyes twinkling. "This sounds like too much fun to waste entirely on you kids."

"Really?" Stevie asked, grinning. "You want to be in on the Swap, too?"

"Absolutely," Max declared. "I'm only sorry that Deborah

is away on assignment all week and will have to miss out." Deborah was Max's wife. She was a newspaper reporter and sometimes had to travel to cover stories. "Stevie, I take it you'll be in charge of this thing?"

"Of course," Stevie said. She glanced around at her friends. "If that's okay with you guys, that is."

The other three girls exchanged glances. "We wouldn't have it any other way," Carole answered for all of them.

"Good," Max said. "Then, Stevie, why don't you see if you can get those name slips made up before class today. You can borrow some paper from my mother. After all, we want to give people enough time to shop." He glanced at his watch. "I'll see you all in the ring in twenty minutes."

"Yikes," Stevie said as Max walked away. "Twenty minutes! How am I supposed to get those name slips done *and* tack up Belle in twenty measly minutes?"

"With a little help from The Saddle Club, of course," Carole spoke up. "Go ahead and do the name slips. If Lisa will help Merrill with Chip, I'll saddle up Belle for you."

"Thanks a million, you guys," Stevie said, throwing her friends a grateful look as she dashed away toward Mrs. Reg's office.

FIFTEEN MINUTES LATER Stevie had finished the name slips and dumped them into a hard hat. Some of the names were a little messy, but she figured people could read them if they tried. Clutching the hatful of names under one arm, she hurried toward Belle's stall. On the way she passed the stall where Rusty, the horse Joe Novick was riding, was stabled. Joe was standing in front of the stall talking with Veronica diAngelo. Or rather *he* was talking and *she* was giggling hysterically, tossing her hair around and fluttering her eyelashes outrageously.

Stevie rolled her eyes. Obviously The Saddle Club had been right about Veronica's crush on Joe. She only hoped he had more sense than to fall for a snob like her.

Just then Joe said something that Stevie didn't hear, but that Veronica apparently thought was the funniest thing anyone had ever said. She let out a loud whoop of laughter, clutching her stomach with one hand and grabbing Joe's arm with the other.

"Oh, Joe!" she shrieked. "You are just *too* funny!"

Stevie groaned and rolled her eyes again. "If that's Veronica's idea of maturity, she can keep it," she muttered. She had never acted that way around Phil, and she never would—no matter how *mature* she got.

She reached Belle's stall and found that Carole had been as good as her word. Belle was almost ready to go. In a matter of minutes, Stevie, Carole, Lisa, and Merrill were in the outdoor ring warming up with the rest of the class—except for one person.

"Is everyone here?" Max asked after a moment, looking around. He frowned. "Where's Veronica?"

"Here I am, Max," Veronica announced, walking into the ring with Danny trailing along behind her. "Sorry I'm late, but it's not my fault. I *told* Red I needed him to saddle up Danny for me, but he was too slow. I finally had to do it myself."

Max sighed. He had learned long ago that it didn't matter how often he yelled at Veronica about doing her own share of the chores; she still insisted on treating Red as though he were her personal groom. "Well, now that you have decided to join us, we can get started," he said drily. "Everybody dismount. I have an announcement about the party on Saturday." He told everyone about the Yankee Swap. "It's a way to help celebrate Joe's and Merrill's birthday, and also a way to reward ourselves for the work we've done. We'll draw names today—everyone should get a gift for the person he or she picks. Make it something fun, don't spend more than ten dollars, and, whatever you do, don't put the person's name on it." He gestured to Stevie.

She stepped forward. "Okay, everyone come pick a name. If you pick yourself, just throw it back. And don't tell anyone who you've got."

The other students hurried up to choose names. Max took one for himself and two to give to Red and Mrs. Reg later.

Carole pulled out a slip of paper and squinted at the name scribbled there. After a moment, she realized it was Joe Novick. "Hmm," she said. Joe could be difficult to buy for—she really didn't know that much about him. This could take some thought.

Meanwhile, Lisa had managed to decipher Stevie's scrawled handwriting and discovered that she had chosen Simon Atherton. She let out a groan. Simon had once had a crush on Lisa, and she didn't want to do anything to start that up again.

When everyone else had chosen a name from the hat, Stevie glanced inside at the slip that was left. "I guess this one's mine," she said. She picked it up and unfolded it, and her heart sank. She had gotten Veronica diAngelo! For a moment she couldn't help wondering if other people had picked her and then thrown her name back in—after all, a couple of people had claimed to have picked their own names and pulled a second slip. There was no way of knowing if they were telling the truth. Still, however it had happened, Stevie was stuck with her choice now. "Whose idea was this Yankee Swap, anyway?" she muttered grumpily. Luckily, no one heard her.

"Quiet down, everyone," Max said after a moment. "You can plan your shopping later. Right now it's time to warm up and then do some more jumping. We'll be working over a slightly more challenging course today, as you can see."

He gestured at the half dozen jumps of various sizes that had been set up. "I want us to start off by going over how to walk a course."

Most of the students already knew how important it was for a rider to walk through a course before riding it. It gave the rider a chance to figure out the best way for his or her horse to approach the jumps—and how many strides of what length that meant taking between fences. It made it less likely that either horse or rider would be surprised in the middle of a round.

After each student had paced off the course several times, Max ordered them to remount. "Okay, now we'll try it," he said. "Lorraine, why don't you go first."

Lorraine nodded and sent Diablo toward the first obstacle. The big bay cleared it handsomely. "Lorraine's an awfully good jumper," Carole commented to Merrill and Lisa as they watched. "It's really her best talent. See her confidence? Even Diablo trusts her."

It was true. Lorraine and Diablo finished the course as well as they had started it.

"Stevie, you're next," Max said.

Stevie urged Belle forward. "Come on, girl," she said to the mare, loudly enough for her friends to hear. "Let's have some fun!"

And they did. Belle practically romped through the course, seeming almost to smile after each fence. If Lorraine and Diablo had been strong and serious performers, Stevie and Belle were accomplished and entertaining.

"What a pair," Lisa commented with a smile. "That's what we were talking about the other day, Merrill—finding a horse that's perfectly suited to you, like Belle and Stevie."

"I see," Merrill said. She smiled as she watched Stevie and Belle take the last fence, but Lisa thought she saw worry in Merrill's eyes.

"What's wrong?" Lisa asked quietly.

Merrill turned to look at her, and Lisa saw that she hadn't been mistaken. Merrill was clearly very nervous, though Lisa couldn't quite understand why. She thought that seeing Lorraine and Stevie go over the course with no trouble would give Merrill more confidence, not less.

"It's just that everyone is doing so well," Merrill replied. "I'm afraid I'm going to mess up again."

Carole had overheard, and she leaned over from her position on Starlight's back. "Don't you like Chip?" she asked anxiously.

"I like him fine," Merrill replied, giving the horse a pat. "I'm sure I could ride him all day on the trail with no trouble at all. But I'm not so sure I can jump on him—or on any other horse, for that matter. I'm afraid I'm just no good at it at all."

Carole and Lisa exchanged worried glances. This was bad news. If Merrill was feeling this nervous, her horse was sure to pick up on it.

"Just try to relax, Merrill," Carole advised, not knowing what else to say. "Pretend nobody is watching you. Just do the best you can. That's all Max expects, and it's all you should expect from yourself, too."

"I'll try," Merrill said, watching as Adam Levine began the course.

Then it was Merrill's turn. She began a slow warm-up lap around the ring. Stevie had ridden back to join her friends, and Carole and Lisa quickly filled her in on what Merrill had said.

"I really hope she does okay this time," Lisa said. "Otherwise there's no telling what she'll do."

"She'll be fine," Stevie said, trying to sound confident. "She can do it—she just hasn't realized it yet."

"Well, I'll be keeping my fingers crossed until she's safely through the course," Carole said, crossing her fingers.

Stevie and Lisa crossed their fingers, too.

Finally Merrill sent Chip toward the first jump. The gelding moved along easily until he was almost there. Then he seemed to sense the hesitation in his rider, and his stride wobbled. He continued on and took the fence, but his approach had been thrown off just enough to make him bring down the top bar. As it clattered to the ground, the gelding came to a halt.

Lisa bit her lip. "Go on, Merrill," she whispered, though of course Merrill couldn't hear her. "Move past it and keep going."

Merrill seemed to be thinking the same thing. She brought the horse under control with her reins and legs, then urged him back into a trot, taking him in a few tight circles and then pointing him toward the next fence. They finished the course without further incident, although Carole suspected that had more to do with Chip's solid training than with Merrill's riding, since the girl was obviously still hesitant and uncertain about what she was doing. There was a distinct look of relief on her face when Chip had cleared the last fence and their turn was over.

"Maybe just having gotten through it will help her state of mind," Lisa whispered as Merrill headed toward them.

"Let's hope so," Stevie said.

But Merrill didn't seem much happier now than when she had started. She brushed aside the other girls' congratulations. "I stunk," she said flatly. "The only reason I made it over anything at all was because Chip did all the work. I just sat there like a sack of potatoes."

"That's okay, Merrill," Carole said. "You're still learning. No one expects you to be a champion."

Merrill just grimaced in reply. It was clear that she didn't feel like talking.

* * *

THE REST OF the day went more or less the same for Merrill. She didn't do anything terribly wrong, but The Saddle Club could tell she wasn't having fun.

By the end of the afternoon's session, even The Saddle Club was glad to dismount and head inside. They were too worried about Merrill to enjoy themselves completely, even though they were all learning a lot.

"How are you doing?" Lisa asked, falling into step beside Merrill as they led their horses down the wide stable aisle.

Merrill looked up. There were tears in her eyes. "I'm quitting," she said, her voice quavering.

"But you can't quit now!" Lisa exclaimed. "If you do, you may never learn to jump."

"That's fine with me," Merrill replied. "There's more to riding than jumping, you know."

"I know," Lisa said. "But jumping is so much fun—I'd hate to think you were missing out on that. I know you could do it if you just gave it more of a chance."

"I've given it a chance," Merrill said. "I've humiliated myself in front of all your friends for two days in a row now. That's plenty."

Lisa thought fast. "At least promise me you'll talk about it with Stevie and Carole before you make up your mind for sure."

"I've already made up my mind," Merrill said. "I might learn to jump someday, but not this week. I'm not good enough for this clinic anyway."

"Of course you are," Lisa said. She had the funniest feeling she was beginning to understand what was bothering Merrill.

It wasn't jumping that scared her—it was being a beginning jumper in front of more experienced riders. Lisa knew that Merrill didn't like feeling conspicuous, and she was bound to feel that way if she thought everyone else in the class was doing better than she.

"I'll still come and watch you guys," Merrill offered. "I just won't take part in the classes. Max probably won't let me come to the party, but—"

"Listen," Lisa interrupted. "I have an idea. I'll meet you at Chip's stall in a few minutes, okay?"

Merrill looked a little confused. "Um, okay," she said.

Lisa hurried Barq along to his stall and quickly untacked him. "I'll be back to give you a good grooming in a minute," she promised, giving him a pat on the nose. Then she headed down the aisle to Starlight's stall.

"Hi, Lisa." Carole was inside the stall, checking Starlight's water bucket. "Are you finished with Barq already?"

"Not exactly," Lisa said. "But I need to talk to you about something. Where's Stevie?" She peered over the half door of Belle's stall, but the mare was alone.

"She went to the tack room," Carole replied. "She'll be back in a second."

"She's back now," Stevie said, coming up behind them. "What's up?"

"It's Merrill," Lisa replied.

"Uh-oh," Stevie said. "Bad news?"

"You bet," Lisa confirmed. "She wants to drop out of the clinic. But I have a plan."

"Let's hear it," said Carole.

Lisa took a deep breath, trying to think of the best way to explain. "We all know that Merrill is a good rider—much better than she thinks she is. Right?"

"Right," Carole said, and Stevie nodded.

"Well, then, it's clear that her jumping problems aren't caused by a lack of skill," Lisa went on. "I think her nervousness has more to do with everyone watching her than with anything else."

Carole shrugged. "That's not good," she said. "If she can't ride in front of other people, that's always going to affect what she can do."

"Not necessarily," Lisa said. "You see, I'm beginning to think that it's only when something is brand new that she has a major problem doing it in front of others. Once she has the hang of something—like riding when she's not jumping—she does fine."

Stevie looked thoughtful. "I never would have thought of that," she said. "But it does make sense."

"What's your plan, Lisa?" Carole asked.

"That's where you come in," Lisa told her. "You're such a good teacher, Carole, I think if you gave Merrill some private jumping instruction tomorrow, she might gain enough confidence to go back to the clinic on Tuesday."

"I'm willing to give it a try if Max says it's okay," Carole said. "Do you think Merrill will go for it?"

"I hope so," Lisa said. "You two will have to help me convince her. It might not be easy."

"We can do it," Stevie said confidently. "Who could turn

down the chance for private lessons from Carole? Come on, let's go find Merrill."

At first Merrill was reluctant to along with the new plan, just as Lisa had feared. But after a few minutes of cajoling from The Saddle Club, she finally gave in.

"All right, all right," she said, interrupting Stevie's lengthy list of reasons why it was important to learn to jump. "I'll try it. I'm not promising I'll go back to the clinic on Tuesday, but I'll give it a try with Carole tomorrow." She smiled at Carole. "Thanks for offering to teach me."

"You're welcome," Carole said, smiling. "I'll go check with Max now and make sure it's okay with him."

THE NEXT DAY Carole headed straight to Pine Hollow after school. Merrill was waiting for her. Carole was relieved—she had been worried that Merrill might back out of the lesson.

"Ready to get started?" Carole asked.

"Ready as I'll ever be, I guess," Merrill said.

"Good. Where's Lisa?" Carole asked.

"She and Stevie are doing some chores," Merrill said. "They said they wanted to stay out of our way."

"Okay then," Carole said. "Wait here—I've got to go find Max. He wanted me to check in about which horse you should ride."

"Won't I be riding Chip?" Merrill asked.

Carole shrugged. "Max said it would depend on which horses his adult class was using."

"Oh, okay," Merrill said. "I'll meet you in the tack room."

"Great." Carole went to find Max. She found him going over some papers in his office.

"Hi, Carole," he said when she came in. "Are you here for Merrill's lesson?"

"Yes," Carole replied. "Can she ride Chip today?"

Max shook his head. "I'm afraid not," he said. "He's out on the trail with the adult beginner class. Everyone in the class showed up today, for a change."

"Oh, well," Carole said. "What about Bluegrass, then? He's easy to handle. Merrill would probably like him."

"He's out, too," Max said. "I told you, the whole class showed up. They took Chip, Bluegrass, Nero, Patch, Harry, and Delilah."

Carole bit her lip. "But Max," she said, "if all the beginner horses are out, who's Merrill supposed to ride?"

"Carole," Max said calmly, "Merrill doesn't need a beginner horse."

"But she's had so much trouble in class—"

Max raised one hand to cut her off. "She's had trouble *jumping* in class," he said. "She hasn't had any trouble at all just *riding*. I've been watching her closely. She's a much better rider than she thinks she is—she can easily handle a more spirited horse than Chip or Bluegrass."

Carole thought about that for a minute, then realized that Max was right. She told him so. "It's not that she has any trouble controlling the horse," she added. "It's *herself* that she has the trouble with, right?"

Max nodded. "And it's your job to help her realize that. You have your work cut out for you."

"I know," Carole said. "But I have to try. So which horse do you think she should ride today?"

"Take your pick," Max said. "Red is riding Topside with the beginners, but most of the others are in."

"Hmm," Carole said, running through the list of possibilities in her mind. Finally she reached a decision. "How about Barq? He's lively but not too hard to control. Plus Merrill has seen him perform beautifully for Lisa in the last two classes. That might give her a little more confidence."

Max smiled. "I think Barq is a perfect choice," he said.

A short while later Carole led Barq, the spirited Arabian gelding, out into the ring. Merrill followed.

"Go ahead and mount," Carole said. "Then take him around the ring a few times."

Merrill swung up into Barq's saddle. Carole watched carefully as the other girl picked up the reins and circled the ring, first keeping Barq to a walk and then to a trot. The horse responded to the command immediately. After a few strides he tried to break into a canter, but Merrill immediately brought him back to a trot. Barq shook his head impatiently, but soon he settled down and waited for his rider's next order. Carole smiled. Max had been right, as usual. Merrill was more than a match for a horse like Barq.

Soon Merrill trotted back over to where Carole was waiting. "What a great horse," she said breathlessly. "He can really move, and his trot is so easy to sit."

"He is wonderful, isn't he?" Carole agreed wholeheartedly. She gave Barq a pat. "He's one of my favorites."

Merrill laughed. "Aren't they all your favorites?"

Carole laughed, too. She was glad that Merrill was in such a good mood. "Very funny. So are you ready to start jumping now?"

Merrill stopped laughing. Her whole body tightened, and Barq shifted nervously beneath her. "I guess so," she said.

"Well, the first thing you can do is relax," Carole instructed her. "I'm not going to send you over any fences just yet." She went over to where the cavalletti were stacked near the stable building. She was going to take it slowly—or as slowly as she could, considering they only had one afternoon. This was the only chance she was going to get to show Merrill how much fun jumping could be.

"IT'S GETTING DARK," Lisa commented to Stevie. "Do you think they're still at it?"

"There's only one way to find out," Stevie said.

The two friends went outside. They reached the gate of the outdoor ring just in time to watch Merrill and Barq make a flawless round over a course of low fences. Barq was moving like a champion, and Merrill rode him confidently, with every move she made helping rather than hindering his progress. They were truly a team.

When Merrill finished, she was beaming. She rode over to the gate and dismounted. Carole, Stevie, and Lisa applauded enthusiastically.

"That was wonderful!" Lisa exclaimed. She gave Merrill a

big hug. Then she turned and hugged Carole. "Carole, you're a miracle worker!"

"She sure is," Merrill agreed. "But some of the credit should go to Barq, too. He's amazing!" She threw her arms around Barq's neck. Then she turned to Lisa. "I have a big favor to ask you," she said.

"What is it?" Lisa asked.

"Can I ride Barq for the rest of the clinic?" Merrill asked.

"Does that mean you're not going to drop out?" Lisa asked. "Then of course you can! I can ride Chip for the rest of the week." She gave Merrill another hug.

"Thanks," Merrill said. "Believe it or not, I'm actually looking forward to class tomorrow. Thanks again, Carole."

Carole smiled. "You just gave me all the thanks I need," she said. "And now let's go shopping."

"Shopping?" Stevie repeated. "Why?"

"For the Yankee Swap, of course," Carole replied. "Since we're going to be awfully busy with the clinic this week, it wouldn't hurt to get it out of the way now."

"I guess that's true," Lisa said, thinking about Simon Atherton. She still wasn't sure what to get him.

Stevie sighed, too. The last thing she felt like doing was shopping for a gift for Veronica the snob. Still, she knew Carole was right. "All right," she said. "Let's get it over with."

Carole was a little surprised at the lack of enthusiasm Stevie and Lisa were showing. "Who did you guys pick, anyway?" she asked.

Stevie shook her head. "We can't tell each other. That would spoil the fun," she said.

"Come on, Merrill," Lisa said. "I'll help you put Barq away. We'll have to hurry if we want to make it over to the shopping center before dinner."

"OKAY, LET'S SPLIT UP," Stevie said when the girls arrived at the shopping center, which was a short walk from Pine Hollow.

"That could be a bit of a challenge," Merrill commented, glancing around at the small selection of shops. "Unless someone is planning to do their gift-buying at the shoe store, that is."

"Hey, you never know," Stevie said. "A shoehorn could make a lovely gift for the right person."

Carole rolled her eyes. "Very funny. Come on, let's get shopping."

The four girls wandered off in different directions. Lisa headed for Sights 'n' Sounds, an electronics store that sold CDs. But as she examined the titles, she realized she had no idea what kind of music Simon liked.

Carole looked through the shelves of the small drugstore but didn't see anything that would make a good gift for Joe Novick. All she really knew about him was that he liked to ride and to play soccer. "That's not much to go on," she muttered, staring at a rack full of stuffed animals.

Meanwhile, Stevie was walking up and down the aisles of the supermarket. "Hmm," she muttered. "Moldy cheese? No, not personal enough. Pickled beets? Nah, too personal. Chicken livers? Too expensive." She sighed. The trouble was, she didn't want to get anything for Veronica. She left the supermarket and went into the variety store next door. As soon as she entered she spotted Merrill, who was standing near the counter looking around in bewilderment.

"How are you doing?" Stevie asked, joining her.

"I don't really know what to get for the person I picked," Merrill admitted. "I guess that's the problem with being a visitor."

"Well, not completely," Stevie said. "I don't know what to get the person I picked, either. This Yankee Swap business isn't as easy as it sounded when I first thought of it."

"I'm sure it will be fun," Merrill said.

"I hope so," Stevie said. She glanced around to make sure Carole and Lisa weren't around. "Listen, I know we're not supposed to tell each other who we picked, but I think we can make an exception in your case. If you want, you can tell me who you have and I'll help you shop." She sighed. "It can't be any harder than my own shopping."

"Thanks, Stevie," Merrill said gratefully. She lowered her voice to a whisper. "I picked Max."

"Max?" Stevie exclaimed with a grin. "That's great! Come on, this should be fun." She began pacing up and down the aisles of the overcrowded shop, which sold everything from water pistols to paper plates to hula hoops.

Merrill followed. "Do you see anything he'd like?" she asked.

Stevie started to shake her head, then stopped in her tracks. "That's it!" she exclaimed, lunging toward an object on a low shelf. "It's perfect!"

LISA HELD HER breath the next day as Merrill took Barq into a trot and rode him toward the first obstacle, a pair of cavalletti set about six inches high. She glanced at Carole and Stevie and saw that they had their fingers crossed.

Barq didn't hesitate at the obstacle. He pricked his ears forward, then gathered himself and took off, clearing it easily. The Saddle Club could see Merrill smiling as Barq landed cleanly and turned toward the next fence.

The rest of the course went just as well. Max had set up several cavalletti jumps as well as some slightly higher fences. He wanted the students to ride through the first part of the course at a trot, then bring their horses to a canter for the larger fences. Barq kept up a brisk trot over the cavalletti, and then, when Merrill signaled, the gelding obediently broke into a smooth canter. He seemed to be enjoying himself as he sailed over the fences. Merrill seemed to be enjoying herself, too. When she finally pulled up at the end, her smile had turned into a full-fledged grin. The Saddle Club cheered as she rode toward them.

"Nice job, Merrill," Max said approvingly. He didn't give direct compliments often, so the whole class knew he really meant it.

Merrill blushed. "Thanks," she said. She looked a little embarrassed, but her friends could tell she was pleased.

It was Carole's turn. She walked Starlight toward the start, passing Max on the way. He winked at her. "Nice job on your part, too, Carole," he said quietly. "You must be some tutor."

Carole felt her face turning as red as Merrill's. "Thanks a lot, Max," she whispered.

AFTER CLASS, LISA untacked Chip and gave him a quick grooming. Then she went to Barq's stall. Merrill was there, carefully combing out Barq's mane. The gelding stood quietly, obviously enjoying the attention.

"Hi, Merrill," Lisa said, leaning on the half door. "Congratulations. You did great today."

"You mean *we* did great today," Merrill corrected, giving Barq a pat. "Barq is incredible. He couldn't have missed a step if he'd tried."

"Well, you deserve credit, too, you know," Lisa reminded her. "You were the one up there telling him what to do—and doing a terrific job of it. I knew that Carole would help. You just needed to get the hang of it."

"Carole's a wonderful teacher," Merrill agreed. "And her lesson made a world of difference. But I think another reason I did so much better today was because of Barq." She took a deep breath. "In fact, I've made a decision. I want my parents to buy him for me."

"What?" Lisa's jaw dropped. "You want to buy Barq?"

"Yes," Merrill said, giving the gelding a hug. "He's the perfect horse for me."

"But . . ." Lisa didn't know what to say. Merrill's announcement had taken her completely by surprise. All she could think was that Pine Hollow without Barq would hardly seem like Pine Hollow at all.

"It makes perfect sense," Merrill went on. "I wasn't sure before what Carole and Stevie meant when they kept talking about how they knew it when they'd found the perfect horse. But now I know. Barq and I did everything right today. I never thought I'd be able to jump like that. I know Barq is for me. I'll call my parents tonight."

Lisa's mind was racing. How could Merrill want to take Barq away from Pine Hollow? "Um, I just remembered," she said. "I promised Stevie and Carole I'd help them with their tack. I'll be back in a minute."

"Okay," Merrill said, turning back to her grooming. As Lisa hurried away, she heard Merrill humming softly to herself while she worked.

She found Stevie and Carole in the tack room. "I've got to tell you guys something!" Lisa exclaimed breathlessly, flopping down onto a trunk.

"What is it?" Carole asked, looking concerned. "Are you all right?"

"I'm fine. It's Merrill who's gone off the deep end," Lisa said. "She's decided on the horse she wants. It's Barq."

Carole and Stevie gasped. "She wants to buy Barq?" Carole exclaimed.

Lisa nodded. "We've got to do something."

"Now, wait a minute, Lisa," Stevie said. "What do you want to do? If Merrill really thinks Barq is the right horse for her, who are we to stop her?"

"But Barq belongs here," Lisa cried. "He belongs at Pine Hollow, not up in Maine."

"Well, we know that all of Max's horses are for sale if someone makes the right offer," Carole reminded her gently. "Barq is special, but Max will sell him if Merrill is serious about buying."

"You can't possibly think this is a good thing, Carole!" Lisa exclaimed.

"No, I don't," Carole said thoughtfully. "I think it's a terrible idea. But I think I have a different reason for thinking that than you do. I'm afraid that Merrill will just be making her riding problem worse."

"What do you mean?" Stevie asked. "Her jumping problem is solved. We saw that today."

"That's not exactly what I mean," Carole said. "I'm not quite sure how to explain it. But it has something to do with what Merrill thinks of herself as a rider."

"I don't get it," Lisa said flatly. "What are you talking about?"

Carole took a deep breath. "Look, we already decided that Merrill's problem with jumping was that she was worried she couldn't do it, and that she was going to look stupid in front of the class. Once she figured out that she *could* do it, she did fine."

"Yeah," Stevie said. "What does that have to do with Barq?"

"Everything," Carole replied. "She's somehow decided that the reason she did well today was that she was riding Barq. If she thinks that's the main reason every time she does well, she's limiting her own abilities in her mind. Do you see?"

"I guess so," Lisa said. "You're saying that Merrill thinks Barq is the magical solution to all her riding problems, and that's a bad thing."

"It sure is," Carole said. "It's nice to have faith in your horse, but it's more important for Merrill to have faith in herself."

Stevie shook her head in wonder. "Since when did you become such a psychologist, Carole?" she teased.

"More like a horse-ologist," Lisa said. "But now that we've figured out the reason why Merrill shouldn't buy Barq, what are we going to do about it?"

"We need a plan," Stevie began, a gleam coming into her eye.

"Hold on, Stevie," Carole said. "I think the first thing we should do is talk to Merrill. Maybe if we point out what she's doing, she'll see reason."

"Hi, girls," a loud, cheerful voice came from the tack-room

doorway. Simon Atherton walked in, almost tripping over the corner of a trunk in his path. "How are you?"

"We're fine, Simon," Carole replied, ignoring Stevie, who was rolling her eyes. "Did you come to clean your tack?"

"No, actually I came to borrow a currycomb," Simon said. "You see, I stuck mine in my pocket after the last class and ended up accidentally bringing it home with me."

"Oh, did you forget to bring it back?" Lisa asked. She was annoyed that Simon had interrupted their conversation, but she didn't want him to see that. After all, it wasn't really his fault.

"Not exactly," Simon said, looking a little embarrassed. "But while it was home, my sister's cat chewed it to bits. He's a bit of a terror—we call him Fang."

The three girls burst out laughing. "Your sister's cat ate your currycomb?" Stevie exclaimed. "Oh, that's a good one!" She chuckled. "Just for that, I'll help you find one you can use. Come on."

As Stevie got up and started rummaging around in the grooming trunk, Carole and Lisa exchanged glances.

"We'll have to figure out what to do about Merrill later," Carole whispered.

Lisa nodded. "I'll talk to her tonight after dinner."

"MMM, THAT WAS delicious, Mrs. Atwood," Merrill said, pushing her chair back from the dinner table. "Thank you. May I be excused? I'd like to call my parents, if that's all right."

"Of course it is, Merrill," Mrs. Atwood replied. "You're excused."

"You can use the phone in our bedroom if you'd like some privacy," Mr. Atwood added.

Lisa looked up, her mouth full of baked potato. She swallowed fast. "Um, Merrill, I wanted to talk to you about something."

"All right," Merrill said. "This call shouldn't take too long. We can talk after that if you want."

Before Lisa could reply, Merrill skipped out of the dining room. A moment later the Atwoods heard her running up the stairs.

"Merrill certainly seems to be in a good mood today," Mrs. Atwood observed.

"Yeah," Lisa replied glumly, pushing the last of her potatoes around on her plate with her fork.

A few minutes later Lisa wandered upstairs. Just then Merrill emerged from Lisa's parents' room, her face glowing.

"Guess what?" she said, running to give Lisa a hug. "They said yes! They're going to call Max tonight to see about a price. Can you believe it?"

"Not really," Lisa muttered, frowning. But Merrill was too ecstatic to notice.

"TODAY, AS YOU can probably tell, we're going to get a little creative," Max announced at the beginning of Thursday afternoon's clinic session.

Lisa looked around the ring and smiled. Max and Red had set up a course that included some very strange-looking obstacles. There was a jump made of logs and brush, one consisting of a large pile of wooden crates, one concocted of some chairs and a couple of broom handles, and one made from old tires.

"The point of this exercise is to get your horses accustomed to jumping anything you ask them to," Max said. "We certainly don't want to scare them, but they need to trust you and do what you say. There's no way of telling what sorts of things you could run across out on the trail—or in a show ring, for that matter."

Lisa knew that was true. She had watched a horse show on TV a couple of weeks earlier and had been surprised at some of the jumps. There had been one shaped like a giant serpent, and one that looked like a tiny castle. Even many of the more normal-shaped fences were painted in wild colors and patterns. Max's jumps weren't that elaborate, but she knew they would serve the same purpose: to test the willingness of the horses to jump anything their riders wanted them to jump.

Most of the horses in the ring, including Chip and Barq, were experienced school horses. They wouldn't have any trouble at all with the new obstacles—they were used to dealing with all sorts of unusual situations. But when Lisa glanced over at her friends, she saw that Stevie and Carole were listening intently. Belle and Starlight were much younger and greener than most of the Pine Hollow horses, and it would be interesting to see how they would handle this challenge.

"All right, Veronica," Max said. "You're up first. Pace the course, then go through it at a slow canter."

As Veronica began pacing off the distances between the jumps, Merrill leaned over to talk to Lisa.

"Guess what Max told me right before class," she whispered

excitedly. "He and my parents have already settled on a price for Barq. That means he'll be able to ship him soon—he'll probably be in Maine in only a couple of weeks. Isn't that great?"

"Uh-huh," Lisa lied with a gulp. There was no time to lose if The Saddle Club was going to talk Merrill out of her plan. "Um, let's talk about it later, okay? You know Max hates it when people talk during class."

"YOU WERE SUCH a good boy," Carole said, giving Starlight a kiss on his soft nose as she finished his grooming. "You didn't let those scary fences stop you at all, did you?" She pulled a few pieces of carrot out of her pocket and fed them to him one by one.

Starlight deserved the treat. He had done very well. Even though Carole had felt him tensing up at each strange obstacle for the first few rounds, he had obeyed her commands and jumped them anyway. That was a tribute to Carole's careful training, as well as to Starlight's character.

Polly Giacomin hadn't fared so well. Her horse Romeo had refused several fences the first time around. With a little help from Max and a lot of patience, Polly had finally managed to get the gelding around the course, but it hadn't been easy.

"Hi, are you almost ready?" Stevie asked, interrupting Carole's thoughts. She leaned on the half door of Starlight's stall. "Lisa and Merrill are just finishing up. Mrs. Atwood will be here soon." Lisa's mother had agreed to drive the girls to the mall for dinner and shopping. So far, Merrill was the only one who had bought a gift for the Yankee Swap.

"I'm ready," Carole said, giving Starlight one final kiss before letting herself out of the stall. "How's Belle?"

"Perfect," Stevie said happily. "She was great today."

"She sure was," Carole said sincerely. Belle had had even less trouble with Max's strange obstacles than Starlight had. If anything, she had almost seemed to be amused by them. Carole shook her head in wonder, thinking again how well matched Stevie and her horse were.

That made Carole think about Merrill and Barq. It would really be a shame if Merrill never got to experience the kind of partnership Stevie had with Belle and Carole had with Starlight. Merrill saw Barq as a wonderful, spirited, obedient horse, but Carole knew that he was that way with almost every rider who climbed on his back. She didn't think he responded any better or any worse to Merrill than he did to the half dozen or so students at Pine Hollow who rode him, including Lisa, Betsy, and Lorraine. Barq was a terrific school horse, but that didn't mean he was the best horse for Merrill to own.

"Oh, there you two are," Lisa said, walking up with Merrill. "My mom just got here. Let's go—I'm starving."

"We're right behind you," Stevie replied, heading for the door. "There's a large everything-on-it pizza at that mall calling our names."

"Everything-but-green-peppers," Carole corrected, hoping a little food would help them figure out how to convince Merrill to leave Barq at Pine Hollow where he belonged.

"MMM, THIS HITS the spot," Stevie said, taking another big bite of her gooey slice of everything-but-green-peppers pizza. The four girls were seated in a comfortable booth in the pizza parlor at the mall. A waiter had just brought over their custom-made pie, fresh from the oven, and the girls were digging in with gusto.

"You're not kidding," Merrill agreed. "All this riding certainly helps you work up an appetite."

"Speaking of riding," Lisa said, wiping a spot of grease from her chin with her napkin, "we kind of wanted to talk to you about something. About Barq, I mean."

"Oh!" Merrill exclaimed. "Did you tell Stevie and Carole about it?" She turned to them. "My parents and Max have already agreed on a price."

"That's exactly what we want to talk to you about," Stevie said. "Are you really sure about what you're doing? About buying Barq, that is?"

"Definitely," Merrill replied. "He's perfect."

"No horse is *perfect,*" Carole said.

"Not even Starlight?" Merrill teased.

Carole smiled. "Well, probably not. He just sometimes seems like it to me."

"It's the same thing with me and Barq," Merrill said, reaching for another slice of pizza. "You know?"

"Still, don't you think you should think about this a little more?" Stevie persisted.

"Why?" Merrill said. "What would be the point? I already know he's the most wonderful horse in the world."

"Well . . ." Stevie glanced at Carole for help. After all, she had come up with the most logical-sounding reasons.

"Well, don't take this the wrong way, Merrill," Carole said, trying to think of the most tactful way to say what she wanted to say. "It's just that we're not sure this is the best thing for you *or* for Barq. You see, you think he's the most wonderful horse in the world right now. But you haven't ridden that many other horses yet. If you limit yourself to Barq now, you may miss out on some other horse who's even better for you."

Merrill was already shaking her head. "I don't think so," she said. "You guys were the ones who told me I'd be able to tell when I found the right horse, right? And you were right. I can do things on Barq that I never thought I'd be able to do. He's the right horse for me, I know it."

"But you don't even know if you can't do those things on another horse," Lisa protested. "Not unless you try."

"I have tried," Merrill said. "I tried on Patch and Chip. Neither one made me feel the way I feel on Barq."

"Listen, Merrill," Carole began slowly. "If you think you can only do well when you're riding Barq, that's not good. You have to know you can trust your own abilities on any horse. Otherwise you'll never be able to advance as a rider."

"I don't really care," Merrill said with a shrug. "I'm not planning to try out for the Olympic Equestrian Team or anything. I have a nice time riding Barq. That's the most important thing to me."

Carole was stumped. It was clear that Merrill would be missing out if she thought Barq was the only horse she could ride well. But how could she make her see that? She glanced over at Lisa, who was looking glum. Carole suspected that Lisa was thinking more about how much she would miss Barq than about how to help Merrill, and Carole couldn't blame her. They would all miss Barq. He was an important part of Pine Hollow.

Just then Stevie finished off the last of her pizza and leaned back with a satisfied sigh. "I'm stuffed," she said, licking some tomato sauce off her fingers.

Carole ignored her. "Merrill," she began again earnestly, "I really think you ought to think about this more carefully. It's a big decision to make so quickly."

"I have thought about it," Merrill said. She pulled a pen out of her jacket pocket and started doodling on her paper place mat. "I've thought about it a lot. Barq is wonderful in every way. He's smart, and well-trained, and I like him."

"But you might like another horse more," Lisa said.

"And you don't want to end up like Veronica diAngelo and Danny, do you?" Carole added.

"What do you mean?" Merrill looked surprised. "Veronica's horse is the best jumper in the whole class. He does everything she asks him to, and more."

Carole nodded. "But does she look like she's having fun riding him?" she asked. "Think about it. As beautifully behaved as Danny is, do you think Veronica really enjoys riding him as much as I like riding Starlight, or Stevie likes riding Belle?" Carole knew the answer to that. Veronica had chosen Danny on the basis of his price and bloodlines, not his personality, and it showed.

Merrill shook her head, looking stubborn. "That doesn't have anything to do with me and Barq," she said firmly. "Barq is the one I want, and that's that."

Carole sighed. She could tell that the discussion was closed, at least for now. But that didn't mean she was giving up—and she knew her friends wouldn't, either.

"Speaking of Veronica," Stevie said darkly, "I can't believe I still haven't thought of a way to get back at her for that sugar trick of hers. I swore I'd get revenge, but what with the jumping clinic and everything, I haven't had time to come up with a plan."

She frowned, thinking how unlucky she was to have ended up with Veronica's name for the Yankee Swap. She hated the thought of spending her hard-earned money on a gift for the snobby girl.

"Especially since she already owns everything in the mall," Stevie muttered.

"What did you say, Stevie?" Lisa asked, watching idly as Merrill sketched a picture of Barq on her place mat.

"Nothing," Stevie said. "I was just thinking about Veronica." There was no way she wanted to get something that Veronica would like—even if she could afford to without a platinum credit card. Suddenly Stevie sat up straight. She had just come up with an idea for revenge. "Hey, Merrill, can I borrow your pen?"

"Sure," Merrill said, passing it over.

Stevie's friends watched as she grabbed a clean place mat from a nearby table and began writing furiously.

"What are you doing?" Carole asked.

"Getting back at Veronica," Stevie announced with a grin, holding up the place mat for her friends to see. She had made it into a sign that read:

ATTENTION ALL STORE OWNERS! BEWARE OF A CUSTOMER NAMED VERONICA DIANGELO. DO NOT ACCEPT HER CREDIT CARD IF SHE TRIES TO BUY SOMETHING WITH IT. HER CREDIT IS NO GOOD. TAKE HER CARD AND CUT IT UP IMMEDIATELY, NO MATTER WHAT SHE SAYS!!

Carole looked perplexed. "What are you doing? Veronica's credit isn't bad."

"I know," Stevie said. "But can't you just see the look on

her face when some salesclerk cuts up her precious credit card?" She grinned. "Now, that's what I call revenge!"

"Um, Stevie," Lisa said. "I'm not sure, but I think what you're doing might be illegal or something. Even if it's not, you could get in an awful lot of trouble."

"Don't be silly," Stevie said with a wave of her hand. "What's illegal about hanging up a sign? Besides, I disguised my handwriting. No one will ever know it was me."

"Where are you planning to hang it, exactly?" Carole asked.

"On the mall directory," Stevie replied. "That way everyone will be sure to see it. Now hurry up and finish eating. I can't wait to hang it up."

She waited impatiently while her friends finished their pizza. Then she led the way out of the restaurant and down the mall to the courtyard near the entrance, where the main directory was located.

"Okay, you guys stand guard while I hang it up," Stevie said. Then she paused. "Wait a second—how am I going to hang it? We don't have any tape . . ." She glanced around, then suddenly lunged for a nearby garbage can. A large wad of sticky pink gum was stuck to the rim. Stevie began picking at it with her fingernails. "Ah-ha! This will do the trick."

"Stevie!" Lisa cried in horror. "Don't touch that! That's disgusting!"

But Stevie ignored her. She pulled a chunk of the gum free and stuck it to the back of her sign. Then she wiped her hand on her jeans and looked around again. Only a few people were sitting or walking nearby, and none of them was paying any attention to the girls. "Okay, the coast looks clear. Keep a lookout and warn me if anyone's coming."

With that, she darted toward the directory, a large plastic-shielded map of the mall. Reaching up as far as she could, she pressed down firmly on the paper above the wad of gum, attaching it to the smooth surface.

"There," she said, hurrying back to join her friends. "Mission accomplished!"

"Not so fast, young lady," boomed a deep voice from behind her.

Whirling around, Stevie saw a burly, bearded man wearing a uniform. He paused long enough to rip Stevie's sign down from the directory, then strode over to the girls.

"What's this all about?" he asked gruffly. He scanned the sign. "Is this some kind of childish joke?"

"Um," Stevie thought fast, but for once her inventive mind failed her. She couldn't think of a single thing to say to talk her way out of this one. "Um . . ."

"Well, if it's a joke, I don't find it very amusing," the guard growled, crumpling up the sign and tossing it into the same trash can where Stevie had found the gum. "And I'll tell you at least one other person who won't think it's funny—the person who's going to have to scrape that gum off the directory, that's who."

"Oh," Stevie said meekly, glancing at the pink smear the sign had left on the plastic. "Sorry about that."

The guard shook his head. "I'm going to let you girls go with a warning—*this time*," he said. "But just remember, if you're old enough to come to the mall by yourselves, you're old enough to stay out of trouble."

"We're very sorry," Lisa spoke up, trying to sound more mature than she felt at that moment. "It won't happen again, we promise."

"It'd better not," the guard said threateningly. He spun around and strode away without another word.

"Whew," Stevie said, sinking down onto a nearby bench. "That was close."

"You're telling me," said Lisa, white-faced.

"Sorry," Stevie said contritely. She frowned. "It's almost like Veronica got the best of us again, though, isn't it?"

"No," said Carole quickly. But she could tell it was too late.

"You know, I'm getting a little sick and tired of Veronica getting the best of me," Stevie declared heatedly. "It's about time she had a taste of her own medicine."

Carole and Lisa exchanged worried glances. They had heard that kind of talk from Stevie before, and it almost always meant trouble.

"She didn't exactly do anything to you just now, Stevie," Lisa pointed out.

"That's not the point," Stevie grumbled. Before anyone could ask what *was* the point, she went on, "I've just got to think of some way to get back at her. Maybe something like tying all Danny's leathers in knots."

"No good," Carole reminded her. "Veronica would just make Red untie them all."

"Hmm. Good point," Stevie said.

"Come on," Lisa said, trying to change the subject. "We'd

better get started on our shopping. The mall closes in less than two hours, and this could be our last chance to look for our Yankee Swap gifts."

The girls headed back through the mall, glancing into stores on their way. Stevie was still muttering about Veronica, but the others did their best to ignore her, chatting instead about the day's class.

"Let's go in here," Carole suggested, stopping in front of a novelty store. "They have all sorts of crazy things."

They went inside. Stevie leaned against a rack full of stuffed animals while the others flipped through some posters. "I know," she said suddenly. "What if I hid Danny's saddle before class on Saturday? Then she wouldn't be able to ride, and Max would yell at her."

"Where exactly were you planning to hide it, Stevie?" Carole asked drily. "In your cubby?"

Stevie shrugged. "I could put it in the grain shed," she said. "Nobody would think to look for it there."

"I hate to say it, Stevie, but it's hardly up to your usual standards," Lisa said. "It almost sounds like something—well, like something Veronica might do to one of us."

Stevie glared at her for a moment, but then her shoulders slumped and she sighed. "I guess you're right," she said. "This can't be any ordinary prank. It has to be something superdramatic—something new and original—a true Stevie Lake extravaganza."

"Well, the only new and original thing I'd like to hear about right now is a new and original idea for a Yankee Swap gift," Carole said, wandering over to a shelf of windup toys. "I don't see anything in here."

"Me neither," Lisa said. "Let's go."

"I noticed a bookstore next door," Merrill said. "Maybe you could find something there."

"That's not a bad idea," Carole said thoughtfully. *Maybe Joe would like a book on soccer*. "Let's check it out."

They headed for the bookstore, with Stevie trailing distractedly behind the others. Once inside, Carole headed for the sports section, Merrill began paging through magazines, and Lisa stood indecisively in front of a table full of bargain books.

"So, are you still not telling who you picked?" Stevie asked her with a mischievous smile. "If you tell me, maybe I could help you find something. I'm good at that—right, Merrill?"

"I'll never tell," Lisa said, glad that Stevie seemed to be thinking about something other than Veronica.

It didn't last long. "Well, maybe I'll go back to the home improvement section," Stevie said. "I might find a book that tells me how to rig it so the bathroom pipes at Pine Hollow empty into Veronica's cubby." She hurried away.

A few minutes later, the four girls reconvened at the front of the store. "Any luck?" Merrill asked the others.

Carole and Lisa shook their heads.

"Me neither," Stevie said. "I thought I had it when one of those books started talking about setting mousetraps. I thought it would be nice if Veronica stuck her hand into her cubby and *snap!* But then the book said most of the traps you can buy aren't strong enough for rats."

Carole sighed. She knew Stevie was just kidding about the mousetrap idea—at least she certainly *hoped* she was—but she still wished her friend would think about something other than getting even. It was getting late, and none of them was having any luck finding a gift.

"Come on," said Lisa, echoing Carole's thoughts. "We'd better keep moving."

They stepped out of the bookstore into the mall corridor and looked around. "Where to next?" Merrill asked.

Stevie was staring into space. "I wonder what Veronica would do if I switched Danny with Nero," she mused. Nero was an old stable horse who had been at Pine Hollow longer than any of the others. "Better yet, I could swap Danny for a rabid bull. That would be great, especially if Veronica actually tried to ride it and . . ." Her voice trailed off and a funny look crossed her face.

"What is it, Stevie?" Lisa demanded. She and Carole had seen that look many times before. It meant that Stevie was up to something.

"Oh, nothing," Stevie said quickly. "Um, I was just thinking that we haven't gotten Merrill a birthday present yet. We should find her something special, just from The Saddle Club. You wouldn't mind if we shopped without you for a while, would you, Merrill?"

"Oh, you don't have to get me anything," Merrill protested, blushing. "Really, it's too much trouble."

"Don't be silly," Carole said. "It's no trouble at all." She had the funniest feeling that there was more on Stevie's mind than a gift for Merrill. But for some reason, it seemed that

Stevie wanted Merrill out of the way for a while. "Why don't you do a little window shopping?" she suggested. "After all, you've already found something for the Yankee Swap. We'll meet you at the entrance in an hour."

Merrill still looked embarrassed, but she reluctantly agreed. As The Saddle Club walked away down the mall, Lisa turned and saw Merrill heading back into the bookstore.

"Okay, Stevie, she's gone," she said. "Now what gives?"

Stevie smiled. "Only the perfect solution to Operation Keep Barq," she announced.

"Really?" Carole said. "Let's hear it."

"Well, as I see it, the main problem is showing Merrill that she can ride and jump just as well on other horses as she can on Barq," Stevie said. "That way she'll see that he's not some kind of magic horse, and she'll want to shop around a little before she decides to buy."

"Sure," Carole said. "*We* all know that. The problem is that Merrill doesn't. She has no interest in trying other horses."

"Right. And like I said before, once Merrill has made up her mind, it's almost impossible to talk her into changing it," Lisa said.

Stevie was still smiling. "Right. So the solution is not to *talk* her into anything," she said. "And that's where my great idea comes in. . . ." Leaning forward, she began outlining her plan to Carole and Lisa.

A few minutes later, The Saddle Club was strolling down the mall again discussing Stevie's idea.

"I think it's our only hope at this point," said Lisa. "And it just might work."

"*Might?*" Stevie repeated, pretending to be hurt.

Carole laughed. "It's unanimous," she said. "Stevie, you make the calls tonight, and we'll try it tomorrow after school. I'll get there a little early and clear it with Max. Lisa, all you have to do is show up with Merrill."

"Got it," said Lisa. "All right, now that that's settled, we still have some shopping to do, and quick." She paused. "And I'm reconsidering what I said about not telling who I picked. I vote that we all tell each other. That way this shopping project can become a Saddle Club project, and maybe we'll actually get it done tonight."

"Agreed," said Carole. "I picked Joe Novick."

Lisa sighed. "You're lucky you got someone normal," she said ruefully. "I got Simon Atherton." She glanced at Stevie out of the corner of her eye, expecting her to laugh. But Stevie just looked glum.

"Who do you have, Stevie?" Carole asked.

"Vrmhmma," Stevie mumbled.

"What?" Lisa said. "Speak up. Who do you have?"

"I said, I have Veronica," Stevie snapped. "Just go ahead and laugh, okay?"

Carole and Lisa did. "Of all the people for you to have picked!" Carole exclaimed.

"Ha, ha," Stevie said sarcastically. "Now stop your giggling and help me think of what to do."

"That could take some thought," Lisa said, still chuckling. "But I do have some ideas for Joe, Carole. Isn't he a big soccer fan?"

Carole nodded. "I thought about getting him a soccer

book, but the only one they had was a big expensive photo book."

"Well, there's just one solution," Lisa said sensibly. "Let's try the sporting goods store."

Moments later The Saddle Club emerged from the sporting goods store. Carole was clutching a bag that contained a World Cup soccer T-shirt. "It's perfect," she said happily. "Now let's work on Simon. What do you think he would want?"

Lisa shrugged. "I don't know," she said. "I really don't know much about what he likes to do outside of Pine Hollow."

"I don't either," Carole admitted. She smiled. "I'm not even sure what he likes to do *at* Pine Hollow, other than bumble around and make a fool of himself."

"That's it!" Stevie exclaimed. "I know what you can get him. Remember the other day when he stumbled over, looking for a currycomb because his sister's cat chewed on his?"

"You think I should get him a new currycomb?" Lisa asked. She shrugged. "It's not very exciting, but I guess it could work."

"Not *just* a new currycomb," Stevie corrected with a grin. "You should get him a new currycomb *and* a cat's chew toy!"

Carole burst out laughing. "It's perfect!" she said.

Lisa agreed. "And the best part is, it's personal without being *too* personal—if you know what I mean."

The others did. They headed for the tack shop, The Saddlery, to purchase a currycomb. While Lisa was picking one out, Carole and Stevie wandered around the store, looking at the merchandise.

"Don't forget, we still have to get something for Merrill, too," Stevie said. "Maybe we can find her something in here."

"I was thinking the same thing, actually," Carole said. "Even if we can convince her not to take Barq, she's going to have a horse of her own soon enough. We could get her something she'll need. Since this is her family's first horse, they won't have anything."

"Well, we can't afford anything like a saddle or bridle, even if we all chip in," Stevie said. "And grooming tools are okay for Simon, but they're a little boring as a birthday gift. What else will she need?"

They thought for a minute, still walking around the shop. Carole stopped in front of a stack of stable blankets.

"Of course," she said, calling Stevie over. "Merrill lives way up north in Maine. Her horse is going to need to keep warm, right?"

"Right," Stevie said, reaching forward to finger the soft wool. "It's the perfect gift." She checked the price and groaned. "Well, who needs an allowance anyway?"

Carole laughed. "It will be worth it," she said. "I'm sure Merrill will love it. It's just too bad we don't know her horse's name—otherwise we could have it monogrammed."

"Why don't we monogram it with her initials?" Stevie suggested. "Then later she can add her horse's name herself if she wants to."

"Sounds good," Carole said.

"What does?" Lisa asked, walking over from the cash register holding a bag.

"We've found the perfect gift for Merrill," Stevie said. She showed Lisa the blankets. "Do you know what her favorite color is?"

"Blue," Lisa said. She smiled. "What a great idea. She'll love it. And I'm sure my parents will chip in on the cost."

"Oh, good," Stevie said with relief. She had been in the process of figuring out how many more weeks she would have to borrow ice cream money from Red to pay for her share of the blanket.

The girls picked out a blue blanket and carried it to the counter. They asked the cashier about monogramming and learned that it could be sent out and done overnight.

"I'm sure my mother can stop by tomorrow and pick it up for us," Lisa said. "Do we have to pay now, or can we pay when we pick it up?"

"You need to put down a deposit now," the cashier said. "Twenty percent."

Digging deep into their pockets, the girls managed to come up with the necessary amount. Stevie was left with just five dollars.

"I don't really want to spend any more than that on Veronica anyway," she said. "This is a much better cause."

The girls thanked the cashier and left the store.

"Now to Pretty Puppy for the second part of Simon's gift," Lisa said. They headed for the pet store across the aisle and found a whole shelf full of cat toys.

"There, that's settled," Carole said, once Lisa had paid for the squeaky rubber mouse she had picked out. "The only one left to buy for is Veronica."

"Let's not and say we did," Stevie muttered. "I still have no idea what to get her."

"Well, let's start at her favorite store," Lisa suggested. "Isn't she always bragging about shopping at Maxwell's?" Maxwell's was a small, exclusive boutique.

As the girls headed toward it, Stevie was still grumbling. "I'd much rather try to figure out ways to make Veronica miserable than what gifts to buy her to make her happy," she said.

"Well, there's no way around it," Carole said. "You've got to get her something, or the Yankee Swap won't work. So concentrate on that and worry about revenge later."

Suddenly Stevie stopped short. "I've got it!" she exclaimed triumphantly.

"What?" asked Lisa. "A gift for Veronica?"

"Yup," Stevie said smugly. "But it's a surprise."

"Hey, no fair," Carole protested.

"Yeah, you already know what we're getting for our people," said Lisa. "You've got to tell us what you're getting Veronica."

Stevie shook her head. "It will be better if it's a surprise to everyone," she said. She gave her friends a pleading look. "Come on, guys. Please?"

Carole and Lisa sighed. "Oh, all right," Lisa said grumpily. "If you're going to be that way about it."

"Let's go find Merrill," Carole added. "We're obviously not needed here."

"Thanks, guys," Stevie called after her friends as they stalked away. She grinned. She could tell they were a little annoyed, but she was sure they'd get over it—especially when they saw her handiwork on Saturday. Whistling softly to herself, Stevie continued down the mall toward Maxwell's.

"ALL THIS JUMPING has been exciting, but I must admit, it will be nice to go on a plain old trail ride for a change," Merrill said to Lisa. It was Friday afternoon, and the girls had just arrived at Pine Hollow.

"I know what you mean," Lisa said, hoisting Prancer's saddle off its rack. "I can't wait to ride Prancer again. I feel like it's been a year instead of just a week."

They headed out into the aisle and parted ways to go tack up their horses. On her way to Prancer's stall, Lisa passed Carole coming out of Starlight's stall.

"Oh, there you are," Carole exclaimed. "We thought you'd never get here. Where's Merrill?"

"Tacking up her dream horse," said Lisa grimly. "I hope this plan works."

"You're not having doubts now, are you?" Carole asked.

"A few," Lisa admitted. "Isn't it possible we could make things worse instead of better?"

Carole shrugged. "I guess it's a risk," she said. "But what choice do we have?"

"You sound like Stevie," Lisa said with a small smile.

"Well, this is her plan," Carole said. "Don't worry, Lisa. Would Max let us do this if he thought it was a bad idea?"

"I guess not," Lisa said. "How much did you tell him, anyway?"

Carole paused. "Just that we were going to take Merrill on a trail ride and, um, encourage her to try out some other horses," she admitted, biting her lip. It wasn't quite the whole truth, and she didn't like lying to Max, even by omission. "He didn't seem worried at all."

"That's all right," Lisa said. "I guess I can do enough worrying for all of us."

Carole nodded. "Me too. I'll see you out front in a few minutes."

Lisa went into Prancer's stall and greeted the pretty Thoroughbred mare fondly. "I've missed you, girl," she whispered, some of her tension melting away as Prancer nuzzled her. "Come on. We're going on a trail ride."

When Lisa led Prancer out to the stable yard, Carole and Merrill were already waiting with their horses. "Where's Stevie?" asked Lisa.

"She's out back helping our, uh, guests unload their horses," Carole replied.

Merrill looked surprised. "Guests? What do you mean?"

"Oh, didn't Lisa mention it to you?" Carole asked, pretending to be surprised. "Stevie hasn't seen her boyfriend Phil in a couple of weeks, so she invited him to ride with us today. His friend A.J. is here, too."

"Oh." Merrill looked a little nervous. "I didn't realize boys would be riding with us."

"Don't worry," Lisa advised. "They're not really like boys. They're just Phil and A.J." Lisa had forgotten how nervous Merrill could be around boys. She hoped it wouldn't interfere with the plan.

"Hi, everyone," Phil said, coming around the corner of the building at that moment. He was leading his horse, Teddy, a handsome bay gelding.

"Everybody ready to ride?" added A.J., who was right behind Phil. A.J., a good-natured red-haired boy, was leading his pretty gray mare, Crystal.

Carole and Lisa greeted the boys and introduced Merrill. A moment later Stevie appeared with Belle in tow. "What are we waiting for?" she demanded immediately. "Let's hit the trail!" She sounded confident, but Carole noticed that Stevie kept her hand on the good-luck horseshoe hanging in the doorway a few seconds longer than she usually did. Carole didn't blame her. They were going to need all the luck they could get.

They rode out of the stable yard with Stevie in the lead. She headed across the pasture just beyond the outdoor ring. A few jumps were set up in the middle of it.

"Hey, look at that," Stevie called back to the others, pulling Belle to a halt. "That must be the course for our last class tomorrow. Max said something about doing some cross-country jumping."

"Must be," Lisa said, nodding.

"Well, let's head for the woods," Stevie said.

"Sounds good. We'll follow you," Carole agreed quickly.

"Hey, that gives me a terrific idea!" Stevie exclaimed. "If you really want to follow me, how about a game of follow the leader?"

"Great idea!" Phil said loudly.

"You mean on horseback?" Merrill asked dubiously.

Lisa nodded enthusiastically. "We play it all the time," she lied. "It's lots of fun. Actually it's more like 'Stevie says' than follow the leader—she calls out orders as we ride and we have to do whatever she tells us to."

Merrill still looked a little uncertain about the whole idea, but before she could say another word Stevie yelled out her first order. "All right, everyone: Trot single file behind me."

With that, she rode through an intricate series of figure eights. The others followed, occasionally becoming confused when they crossed paths and got in each other's way, but laughing all the time.

"Now for a more challenging move," Stevie announced. "Everybody walk. No stirrups!"

For a few more minutes, Stevie led everyone through different moves and gaits. She even led them over a couple of the jumps. Then she brought Belle to a stop and slid off her back.

"Now it's time for some real fun," she said. "Dismount and form a circle." In a matter of seconds, the riders had their horses arranged in a slightly lopsided circle. "Everyone switch horses with the person to their right!" She glanced over at Merrill, who was to her left. "That means Belle is all yours for this round, Merrill."

Merrill looked decidedly nervous. "I don't know about this—"

But before she could finish her protest, Phil had stepped over and grabbed Barq's reins from her. "He's all mine now," he said with a grin, swinging up into the saddle.

Merrill bit her lip and opened her mouth as if to say something. Then she snapped it shut again and stepped over to Belle. Giving the mare a slightly nervous pat, she put one foot in the stirrup and mounted.

As she reached for Starlight's reins, Lisa whispered to Carole, "I think it's lucky that Merrill is kind of intimidated by strange boys. My guess is she didn't want to argue with Phil about making the switch."

Once everyone was mounted on their new horses, Stevie urged Crystal into a trot. "Pay attention," she called. "It's time to have some fun!"

Carole, who was now riding Teddy, kept a close eye on Merrill as the group followed Stevie through another set of paces. The other girl's shoulders looked a little tense for the first few minutes, but then she seemed to relax as Belle pranced her way through the moves. Carole breathed a sigh of relief. She hadn't wanted to think about what would have happened if Merrill had flatly refused to go along with this. She hoped things would continue to go smoothly.

"Okay, pay attention," Stevie said, turning Crystal around to face the others, who quickly formed another circle. "It's time for another switch. This time trade horses with the person directly across from you."

"That's you and me, Merrill," Lisa called, sliding off Starlight's back and leading him over to Belle. "Have fun with Starlight. He's a dreamboat."

Before Merrill could say a word, Lisa snatched Belle's reins and quickly mounted. Merrill was left staring up at Starlight, who stared back down at her calmly. With a sigh, she swung into his saddle.

"Riders up," Stevie yelled. "Follow me."

After a few minutes of simple moves, Stevie glanced back over her shoulder. "Okay, now spread out," she ordered. "We're going to jump." She urged Teddy into a slow canter and headed for the first fence.

Lisa glanced at Merrill, whose face had turned white. She knew that this was the true test. Would Merrill refuse to jump on a strange horse? Worse yet, what would happen if she tried to jump and did badly?

Lisa held her breath as Carole jumped the fence after Stevie. It was Merrill's turn. For a moment, Merrill looked indecisive, and Lisa was sure she was going to refuse to make the jump. But, luckily, Starlight's youth and equine nature—to say nothing of his love of jumping—took over. Without any urging from his rider, he broke into a canter and headed for the fence. Merrill didn't encourage him, but she didn't try to stop him, either, and before Lisa knew it, Starlight had cleared the fence easily. Lisa felt like cheering. She took her turn over the fence and trotted over to join Merrill, who still looked a little anxious. "Hey, you looked great going over that fence," Lisa said encouragingly. "I guess all the work we've been doing in the jumping clinic is really paying off."

"I guess," Merrill replied. "But I hope Stevie doesn't make us jump anymore."

Lisa bit her lip. Apparently Merrill wasn't won over to the joys of jumping on other horses yet. "How do you like Starlight?" she asked.

Merrill looked surprised, as if the question hadn't even occurred to her. "Oh!" she said. "Actually, he's great. His gaits are really smooth."

"Okay, everyone, pay attention!" Stevie called at that moment. "Time to swap again!"

This time, Merrill ended up riding Crystal, A.J.'s gray mare. Stevie didn't wait as long before leading the group to the jumps. And this time Merrill looked less nervous about jumping. Crystal, who was very well trained, cleared every fence like a pro.

At the next switch, Merrill got Teddy. This time, when Stevie headed for the jumps, Merrill seemed almost relaxed. In fact, she seemed to be enjoying riding Teddy a lot. Stevie noticed and made this round a long one.

"All right," Stevie called at last. All the riders halted and waited for her next order. "How about one more switch? Everyone move one horse to the left."

Merrill dismounted reluctantly and handed Teddy's reins to Carole. Then she looked left, and Lisa saw her gulp. The horse standing there was Prancer. All the rider-switching had gotten the high-strung Thoroughbred rather excited, and she was stamping one foreleg and tossing her head restlessly.

Stevie noticed, too, and she glanced at Carole anxiously. Carole watched Merrill and Prancer carefully as Merrill took the reins and patted the mare on the neck, trying to calm her down. Then Carole took a deep breath and nodded briefly.

"Everyone in the saddle," Stevie said. If Carole thought Merrill could handle Prancer in her high-strung state, that was good enough for Stevie. She knew Carole wouldn't willingly put a horse or rider in danger. "Let's go."

Merrill mounted along with the others and quickly brought Prancer under control, although the mare still looked a bit skittish. Stevie led the riders along on the flat for quite a while this time, keeping an eye on Merrill. Finally, when she felt she had stalled long enough, she led the group toward the jumps again. She took Starlight over the first two fences, then turned him in a wide arc and pulled up so she could watch the others go over. Carole was first on Crystal; then A.J., Phil, and Lisa each jumped.

Then it was Merrill's turn. She signaled to Prancer and the mare cantered toward the first fence, moving a little faster than she should have. Merrill leaned forward into jumping position as Prancer closed in on the fence.

Stevie held her breath. She could tell that Prancer was moving too fast—there was no way she could make a smooth jump this way. The Thoroughbred seemed to know it, too. Her gait became choppy, and she came almost to a stop just in front of the fence, nearly unseating her rider. Merrill grasped at Prancer's mane as the mare took off from an awkward standstill, her heels clipping the top rail as she hopped over the fence and landed heavily—but safely—on the other side.

"Oh, no," Lisa whispered, her hands twisting in Barq's mane as she watched from behind. The plan had been going so well, but this was sure to spook Merrill badly. They would be lucky if Merrill would ever jump again on Barq, let alone on any other horse.

But Merrill surprised them all. With a look of determination, she clucked loudly to Prancer, getting the mare's attention as she gathered up the reins and signaled with her legs. Obediently, Prancer recovered her gait and cantered forward toward the second fence.

"She's going on!" Carole exclaimed to Stevie in surprise. "She's going for it!"

"I know," Stevie replied, her eyes glued to Merrill and Prancer. "Just watch!"

Prancer cantered toward the second fence, her strides coming more evenly now. She approached in perfect position, gathered herself for the jump, and, in one smooth movement, cleared the fence with inches to spare.

Without realizing they were doing it, Carole, Stevie, and Lisa broke into cheers. Phil and A.J. joined in.

Merrill trotted over to them, looking a little surprised as she swung down from the saddle. "What?" she said. "What's going on?"

Lisa smiled at her. "I guess it's about time we told you."

A few minutes later all was explained. "So you guys went to all this trouble just for me?" Merrill said, looking astonished. "I mean, I had the feeling *something* weird was going on, but I wasn't sure what."

"We didn't want you to go home thinking you could only

jump well on Barq," Carole said. "We wanted you to know that your abilities weren't necessarily connected to a particular horse."

"Well, I guess I know that now," Merrill said, stroking Prancer on the nose. The mare had calmed down, and she nuzzled Merrill in a friendly way. "If I could get Prancer over that second jump, I guess I'm ready for just about anything."

Lisa laughed in surprise and delight. It was the most self-congratulatory thing she had ever heard Merrill say—and it sounded awfully good to Lisa. "I guess you are," she agreed whole-heartedly.

"Well, we were impressed," Phil put in, and A.J. nodded.

"You're just saying that to butter her up so she'll still let you come to her birthday party tomorrow night," Stevie teased.

"Come on, everyone," Carole said. "We'd better start walking these horses while we talk. Stevie's been working them hard, and we don't want them to stiffen up, or Max may never let any of us ride again."

They walked the horses back to the stable. Merrill and Lisa walked next to each other so they could talk.

"Do you still want to buy Barq?" Lisa asked a little shyly.

Merrill shrugged. "I don't know. I still think Barq is great," she said, glancing at the big bay horse walking calmly beside her. "But I'm not so sure anymore that he's the only horse for me."

Lisa smiled. "I'm glad to hear you say that."

"Really?" Merrill said. "You don't think I should buy him?"

Lisa shook her head. "At first it was because I was just being selfish," she admitted. "I didn't want Barq to leave Pine Hollow. Even though I mostly ride Prancer now, I would have missed him a lot. But then I started listening to what Carole was saying, and I realized there was an even more important reason to talk you out of buying Barq."

"Because it wouldn't be good for me," Merrill guessed.

"Right. And then I started thinking about when I first started riding," Lisa continued. "I rode Patch for my first lesson at Pine Hollow, just like you. But pretty soon after that I switched to a horse named Pepper."

"I remember you writing about him," Merrill said, nodding.

"I loved Pepper a lot, and I loved riding him," Lisa said. "I don't regret for a second the time I spent with him—he taught me so much. When he retired, I didn't know what I was going to do. I tried a couple of other horses who didn't really suit me. Then I started riding Barq."

"And he did suit you," Merrill guessed.

"He sure did," Lisa said. "And then Prancer came to Pine Hollow, and she suited me even better. So I guess what I'm trying to say is even though I still miss Pepper, I'm glad I've had the chance to discover how wonderful other horses can be to ride, too."

"I think I see what you're saying," Merrill said slowly. "And I think you may be right. Lisa, I don't know how I get along without you in Maine. You always know how to get me to look at things in a different way. Just like that time in speech class, remember?"

Lisa smiled. "Does this mean you're definitely not buying Barq?"

"It does," Merrill said. "I shouldn't rush into things by

buying him just because he was the first horse I felt confident jumping on." She blushed. "Now that I think about it, I don't think I gave Carole's teaching enough credit for that," she admitted. "I think I would have felt comfortable on almost any horse after she was through with me. I just didn't realize it until now."

"Don't worry," Lisa said. "I think Carole has known that all along."

"Anyway, after riding all these different horses today, I think I can find one that's *really* right for me. I liked Teddy a lot, and Starlight, too."

Lisa laughed. "I don't think either one of them is for sale," she teased.

Merrill laughed, too. "Too bad," she said. "But my perfect horse is out there somewhere—and half the fun is going to be finding him or her when *I'm* ready."

"Definitely," Lisa said.

"UP AND AT 'em, birthday girl! Rise and shine!" Stevie sang into Merrill's ear.

Merrill groaned and rolled over. But when Stevie, Carole, and Lisa burst into a rousing rendition of "Happy Birthday," she had no choice but to sit up.

"What time is it?" she mumbled when they were finished singing.

"Time to get up," Lisa said. "The final clinic class starts in two hours, and my mom has been slaving over a hot stove all morning cooking up a special birthday breakfast."

"Oh, I hope she didn't go to too much trouble," Merrill said.

Stevie rolled her eyes. "Oh, please," she said. "It's your birthday. Do what I always do: Take advantage of it!"

Merrill yawned and climbed out of bed. "We shouldn't have stayed up so late talking," she said. "I could sleep for another six hours." The girls had had a sleepover and had stayed up past midnight.

"I've got bad news for you, then," Carole said. "You won't be sleeping again for quite a while. We've got a big day ahead of us."

"Right," Stevie said. "First your birthday breakfast, then the clinic, then the party!"

Merrill sniffed at the aromas that drifted up to them from the kitchen. "Hey, is that banana pancakes I smell?" she said, starting to look a little more awake.

"They're still your favorite, aren't they?" Lisa asked.

"They sure are!" Merrill exclaimed, throwing on her robe and heading for the door. "Come on, what are you all waiting for? Let's eat!"

After the girls had all eaten so many of Mrs. Atwood's fluffy banana pancakes that they could hardly move, Mr. Atwood got up and left the room. He returned a moment later, holding two beautifully wrapped packages. He set them on the table in front of Merrill.

"Merrill, we're so glad you're here to share your birthday with us," Mrs. Atwood said, pushing the smaller package toward her. "This gift is from Mr. Atwood and me. We hope you like it."

"Oh, thank you," Merrill said shyly. "You really didn't have to get me anything. Just letting me stay here this week has been enough of a gift."

Mr. Atwood smiled at her. "We know we didn't have to," he said. "But we wanted to. Go ahead, open it."

Merrill carefully unwrapped the gift. Inside the paper was a cardboard box. When Merrill lifted the lid, she gasped.

"Oh, it's beautiful!" she exclaimed, pulling out a silver charm bracelet. There were three charms on it—one in the shape of Maine, one in the shape of Virginia, and the third in the shape of a tiny horse.

"Somehow those charms seemed appropriate," Mrs. Atwood said.

"Oh, they are! Thank you so much, Mr. and Mrs. Atwood. I love it!" Merrill held out her arm so Lisa could fasten the bracelet on her. Then she held it up and watched the charms sparkle in the morning sunlight streaming through the dining room window.

"Now ours," Stevie demanded impatiently, shoving the larger package toward her.

Merrill picked it up and squeezed it. "Hmm, it's soft. Is it something to wear?" she guessed.

The Saddle Club shared a grin. "Sort of," Carole replied mischievously.

Merrill quickly unwrapped the present, revealing the blue wool horse blanket with the initials "MM" stitched on the side in white thread. "But what . . . ," Merrill began, looking confused.

"It's a horse blanket," Lisa explained quickly. "For when you finally get your dream horse."

"So your dream horse doesn't freeze up there in Maine," Stevie added.

Merrill laughed. "How perfect!" she cried. "What a great gift. You guys are the best."

"So are you," Lisa told her, getting up to give her a hug. "Happy birthday."

A LITTLE LATER that morning the girls gathered in the outdoor ring with the rest of the class, waiting for Max to begin the last session of the clinic. They had already dropped their carefully wrapped Yankee Swap gifts into the large cardboard box Mrs. Reg had put in the main aisle of the stable. Stevie, secretive to the end, had waited until the others had left the room before adding hers to the pile.

"I can't believe it's almost over," Joe Novick commented.

"Me too," Merrill said. "I can't believe I almost dropped out."

"You did?" Joe asked. "Why?"

Merrill shrugged. "I didn't think I was good enough," she said softly.

Joe smiled at her. "Well I for one am glad you stuck with it," he said.

Before Merrill had to think of a response to that, Max stepped into the ring. "All right, everyone," he said. "Ready to ride?"

For the next few hours, there was no more time to talk as Max put them through their paces. As Merrill took Barq over fence after fence throughout the day, Lisa noticed the blissful look on her face. She knew what it meant: Merrill had finally found out what it felt like to fly.

* * *

"OKAY, THAT'S A WRAP," Max announced at last. "Everybody inside. Make your horses comfortable, then reconvene in the indoor ring."

The riders obeyed. A short while later, when they stepped into the indoor ring, they found it transformed. Several round tables were set up for dinner at one end, complete with colorful paper tablecloths. At the other end of the ring was a table containing a large CD player and piles of CDs.

"Wow," Stevie commented as she took it all in.

"Ladies, please take a seat," said Red O'Malley, materializing behind them. He was dressed in a white waiter's apron and carrying a pad and paper. Then he hurried off to the next group of students.

"I feel a little underdressed," Lisa said, looking down at her jeans and sweater.

Stevie looked up as Max entered the room. She grinned. "Well, if we're underdressed, I think Max is a little *over*dressed for the occasion!"

The others looked up and laughed. Max was wearing a tuxedo! "What's going on here, anyway?" Carole asked.

Max didn't leave her in suspense for long. "Could I have your attention, please," he called, stepping in front of the tables, where all the riders had found seats. "Welcome to the Pine Hollow Club. I will be your host for the evening. In just a moment we'll begin our awards ceremony. Until then, just sit back, relax, and enjoy the refreshing beverages our waiter will be bringing around."

On cue, Red stepped into the ring carrying a large tray full of sodas, which he began distributing.

"Awards ceremony?" Lisa commented. "Max didn't tell us anything about that."

"I'm getting the funniest feeling that there are a lot of things Max didn't tell us about," Carole replied as Red set an ice-cold glass of cola in front of her. She took a sip. "I guess all we can do is what he said—sit back, relax, and see what happens next."

Stevie rolled her eyes as she watched Veronica, who was sitting at a nearby table. "Well, I think Max has convinced at least one person that she's in a four-star restaurant," she commented. "Veronica just complained to Red that her diet cola had a lemon slice in it instead of a lime."

Soon Max returned to the ring. "And now, ladies and gentlemen, for the awards portion of our show," he proclaimed. "Mother, the envelope please."

Mrs. Reg entered the ring and handed Max a large, bulging manila envelope. Max reached inside and pulled out a handful of blue show ribbons.

"For our first award this evening, I'd like to present a blue ribbon for Most Attentive Student," he announced. "This honor goes to the rider who paid attention throughout the week, obeyed instructions to the letter, and never, ever whispered to his or her friends while I was speaking." He paused dramatically. "And the winner is . . . Lorraine Olsen! Lorraine, come on up here and accept your prize."

Lorraine jumped up from her seat and went to get her ribbon. She held it up with a smile, gave a little bow, then returned to her table.

"Congratulations, Lorraine," Max said. "Next we have the

prize for the *Least* Attentive Student. This goes to the rider who almost always seemed to have something important to discuss during class."

Stevie stood up and headed for Max before he even called her name. She grinned good-naturedly. "Thanks, Max," she said. "This is such an honor. Do I get to make a speech?"

Max rolled his eyes. "I think we've heard enough of your speeches lately, Miss Lake," he responded gruffly. But his eyes were twinkling, and he gave Stevie a wink as he handed her the blue ribbon.

Max went on to pass out more awards, some serious and some silly. Soon almost everyone in the class held a blue ribbon. Carole won for being the Best All-Around Jumper. Lisa took the prize for Most Considerate. Simon won the Weakest Glue in the Saddle award, since he had fallen off Bluegrass several times during the course of the week. Veronica accepted the award for Best-Trained Horse; Adam Levine won Best Form for his jumping position; and Joe took the blue for Most Precise for the accuracy of his pacing. Polly Giacomin won a ribbon for Best-Dressed Horse—her gelding, Romeo, had a fancy red monogrammed saddle pad. Meg Durham, who had been fighting a cold all week, won The Show Must Go On award; and Betsy Cavanaugh won a blue for Most Giggling.

"That's one award that's certainly deserved," Stevie whispered to her friends as Betsy went up to accept her ribbon, giggling wildly all the way.

"And now," Max said, when there was only one blue ribbon left in his envelope, "we have the most important award of all. This is the one that demonstrates why intensive clinics like this are important. It's the award for Most Improved."

Carole, Stevie, and Lisa turned to look at Merrill, but she didn't seem to notice. She was watching Max attentively.

"This award goes to the student whose jumping has improved the most dramatically over the past week," Max went on. "The rider I'm talking about started this week so nervous about jumping that she could hardly look at a fence without shaking. I wasn't sure she was going to make it through the clinic, and I suspect she wasn't sure, either."

By this time, everyone in the room was looking at Merrill.

"But by today, she was jumping as if she'd been doing it all her life," Max declared. "She has made great strides this week, and I'm glad she stuck with it. Merrill Minot, come on up here and get your ribbon."

Merrill blushed and stood up. She walked over to Max and shyly accepted the ribbon. "Thanks, Max," she whispered.

"You're welcome, Merrill," he replied. "Nice work." Seeing how uncomfortable she was with all the attention, Max allowed her to hurry back to her table, where The Saddle Club greeted her with congratulations and pats on the back. Merrill accepted both happily.

"That's it for the awards," Max said. "Now let's eat!"

"Thank goodness," Stevie declared, as Red and Mrs. Reg entered with trays piled high with fried chicken, mashed potatoes, homemade cornbread, and all sorts of other good things. "I'm so hungry I could eat a horse!"

AFTER EVERYONE HAD eaten, Max stepped to the center of the ring again. "Now we have a special treat," he said. "Just when you thought you couldn't eat another bite, you're going to have to find room somewhere, because . . ."

He gestured to the door. Mrs. Reg entered, bearing a huge, white-frosted cake on a silver tray. She carried it over to the table where The Saddle Club was sitting. Written on the top of the cake in icing were the words HAPPY BIRTHDAY MERRILL AND JOE. Mrs. Reg pulled a book of matches out of her pocket and started lighting the candles, which formed a ring around the letters.

"We're celebrating a couple of birthdays today," Max said. "Joe, pull up a chair. You and Merrill are going to have to work to blow out all of those candles."

Joe grinned and obeyed, dragging his chair over to the table and inserting it between Merrill and Lisa. "I'm ready when you are, Merrill," he announced when all the candles had been lit.

Merrill was blushing again, but she was smiling, too. "I'm ready," she said.

"Okay, then, on the count of three," Max said. "One . . . two . . . three . . . blow!"

Merrill and Joe blew out all the candles in one try.

"I hope you made a wish!" Stevie cried.

Joe smiled at Merrill. "I did," he replied. Only Merrill's friends could tell that the already pink-cheeked Merrill turned even pinker.

"Okay, everybody, line up," Mrs. Reg said. She stepped forward with a cake knife and began cutting large slices.

"Now," Max began, when everyone was munching happily on the delicious cake, "it's time for something I'm sure you've all been waiting for. In honor of our birthday girl and boy, and thanks to our tireless planner of party fun—Stevie Lake—it's time for the Yankee Swap!"

Everyone headed for the wide main aisle, where they had left their wrapped gifts. Red dragged the box into the center of the aisle. Stevie hurried forward to help him take out the gifts, which were all sorts of interesting shapes and sizes, and arrange them so everyone could see.

"Come on, sit down in a circle," Stevie directed the other students. "You too, Max, Red, Mrs. Reg. You wanted to be part of this, you know."

"We wouldn't miss it for the world," Mrs. Reg said. She had

dragged a chair from one of the tables in the ring. "But no sitting on the ground for me. I'm not as young as the rest of you, you know."

Soon they were ready to start. Stevie quickly explained the rules once again. "So once you've chosen your gift and unwrapped it, you decide whether you want what you've picked or if you'd rather trade with someone else who has already picked. Then you just have to wait and see whether you get to keep what you chose," she said. "Anyone who picks after you can decide to trade with you if they want to. So you really never know what gift you're going to end up with. Everybody get it?"

"Got it," several people responded.

"Good," Stevie said. "Now for the order. Plain old alphabetical is so boring, don't you think? Besides, we don't want Max to be able to go last and have his pick of the prizes. So I have a better idea. We'll go in reverse alphabetical order according to *first* names."

"So where does that put me?" Mrs. Reg asked mischievously.

Stevie realized that none of them knew Mrs. Reg's first name. And she could tell by the grin on the woman's face that she wasn't about to tell. Stevie thought fast. "Why, between Polly and Merrill, of course," she said calmly. "For 'Missus.' "

Everyone laughed, Mrs. Reg loudest of all. "That works for me," she declared.

"Great," Stevie said. She smiled sweetly at Veronica. "That means you go first, Veronica."

Giving Stevie a suspicious look, Veronica tossed her long,

straight hair behind her shoulder. Then she leaned forward to examine the selection of gifts. "Oh, this one looks good," she said, reaching for a package in the middle of the pile. It was beautifully wrapped in the distinctive gold and white paper of Maxwell's Boutique. "Maxwell's is my favorite store," she added smugly, ripping away the paper.

Veronica opened the white box underneath the paper and peeked inside expectantly. Then her face darkened into a frown. "What's the big idea?" she demanded, narrowing her eyes and staring at Stevie.

"What do you mean, Veronica?" Stevie asked, playing innocent. "What did you get?"

Veronica turned the box over and dumped its contents out. Onto the floor tumbled a large, black, dirty lump of coal.

The other students burst into laughter. That made Veronica frown even harder. "You're responsible for this little joke, aren't you, Stevie Lake?" she demanded icily.

Stevie just grinned. "You know we're not supposed to tell which gift we brought until the end," she said. "But I guess this should teach you not to judge a gift by its packaging, right, Veronica?" Ignoring the other girl's baleful glare, she turned away. "Okay, I guess I'm next, right?"

She grabbed one of the gifts from the pile and tore off the paper. Inside was a rolled-up poster. "Hey, great," she said. "I hope it's a . . ." Her voice trailed off as she unfurled the poster and saw the leaping ballerina pictured on it. "Oh, um, well, it's very nice," she finished lamely. Stevie was not a big ballet fan. Still, she knew that someone would probably trade with her for it—Lisa had taken ballet lessons for a few years, and Meg Durham was still taking them. "Simon, you're next."

Simon Atherton peered at the pile of packages. "Gosh, this is a hard decision," he exclaimed. "They all look so beautiful. Well, here goes." He picked up a rectangular package wrapped in blue paper and opened it.

"What is it?" asked Stevie eagerly.

Simon held it up. It was a paperback book called *Advanced Training Methods*. "Somehow I don't think this is the gift that was intended for me," he joked. Simon was the newest rider in the entire class, and he certainly wasn't ready for any advanced training.

"Don't worry, Simon," said Max. "I'm sure someone will want to trade you for that." He glanced at Carole, who was staring at the book eagerly. "Who's next? Red, I think it's you."

"Wait a minute," said Simon. "I want to trade . . . with Stephanie."

Stevie looked surprised. "Are you a ballet fan, Simon?" she asked.

He shrugged. "No. But my sister might like it. And *nobody* in my family is an advanced rider."

Stevie tossed Simon the poster. "Go ahead, Red," she urged.

Red made his selection quickly. He unwrapped a brightly wrapped package that turned out to contain a roll of 35 millimeter film and a pretty picture frame. He shrugged. "Well, I do have a camera," he said. "At least I think I do. I haven't used it in a while."

"Do you want to trade with me or Simon, Red?" Stevie asked eagerly. "Oh, or with Veronica?" She knew that the game was more fun when there was lots of trading. She was also hoping that nobody would offer to trade with Veronica. She had the funniest feeling she was pretty safe in that hope.

Red shook his head. "I think I'll stick with the film for now."

It was Polly's turn next. She grabbed a small, square gift wrapped in pretty floral paper and tied with a big bow. Opening the box inside, she pulled out a mug. "Hmm," she said. "I'm not sure this gift is me." She held up the mug so everyone could see. Printed on it was "#1 Mom."

"Well, I guess we all know who that gift was meant for," Carole commented with a smile. Mrs. Reg was the only mother in the room.

"I'm going to trade," Polly announced, putting the mug back in its box. "Red, hand over that film."

"You mean I'm the number-one Mom?" Red asked, accepting the box that Polly handed him. "I'm so touched."

"Go ahead, Mrs. Reg, it's your turn," Carole said.

Mrs. Reg examined the remaining gifts for a moment and then leaned forward to pick up a flat rectangular one. Carole gasped as she recognized her gift for Joe Novick. Somehow she couldn't picture Mrs. Reg wearing the brightly colored World Cup T-shirt.

Apparently nobody else could, either, because everyone laughed when she pulled it out of the box. "Oh, it's lovely," she said, holding it up against her. "But look, it's not my size," she added, pretending to be disappointed. "I guess I'll have to trade." She glanced around the circle. Everyone waited for her to reach for the mug, but instead she nodded at Simon. "I'll take that ballet poster, Simon," she said, handing him the T-shirt. "I hope your sister won't be too disappointed."

Stevie watched as Simon took the shirt and passed the poster to Mrs. Reg. "Next—" she began, but Mrs. Reg interrupted.

"Wait a minute here," she said. "It's still my turn. I think I'll make another trade. Is that allowed?"

Stevie shrugged. "I don't see why not," she said. "Like you said, it's still your turn."

"Good," Mrs. Reg said with a smile. "Then I think I'll take that mug. Sorry, Red. But at least you get this lovely poster in return."

"Terrific," Red replied, making the exchange. "I'll have to hang this up on the door of the closet where I keep my tutu."

"Your turn, Merrill," Stevie said. "Go ahead, and make sure you pick something good. It's your birthday, after all."

Merrill picked a package that turned out to contain two pairs of brightly colored socks. One of them was black with bright green horses, and the other was hot pink with orange and purple swirls.

"Gee, I wonder who those are meant for," Lisa commented, glancing at Betsy, who was wearing purple and yellow polka-dot socks under her sneakers.

"Do you want to trade with someone, Merrill?" Joe asked.

Merrill shook her head. "I'll stick with the socks for now," she replied. Lisa suspected that Merrill's shyness prevented her from making a trade—she had been eyeing the ballet poster admiringly—but she didn't say anything to change her mind. There was only so much The Saddle Club could do to try to make Merrill bolder, and they had already made great progress in the last week. There was no point in embarrassing her by insisting she make a trade.

"I'm next, right?" Meg spoke up eagerly. She chose a package wrapped in shiny blue and white paper. Inside were several tubes of oil paint. Meg looked perplexed. "Paint?" she said. "Who is this for?"

Stevie shrugged. As far as she knew, nobody in the room was a serious painter. If she hadn't been sure Simon had been the one to buy Mrs. Reg the silly #1 Mom mug, she would have suspected him of buying the paint. He was always a few steps behind everyone else, and was more likely than anyone else to pick an inappropriate gift. "Do you want to trade it away?" she asked Meg.

"As a matter of fact, I do," Meg declared. "Red, sorry to do it, but I want that ballet poster. It's of my favorite dancer." She gave him an apologetic smile. "Sorry to stick you with the paint."

"That's quite all right," Red said, catching the paint tubes as she tossed them to him. Lisa thought he looked pleased with the trade.

"Do you do any painting, Red?" she asked curiously.

"As a matter of fact, I have been known to dabble," he replied shyly.

"Dabble?" Betsy exclaimed. "Don't be modest, Red. He's a great artist! You should see some of the paintings of horses he's done."

"Really?" Stevie said, looking at Red with new interest. She hadn't known about this side of him. Luckily, whoever had drawn his name—and she strongly suspected it was Betsy—*had* known. That was another great thing about this game. You never knew what you were going to find out about the people you played with. "Max, you're next."

"Well, let's see," Max said, glancing over the diminished pile of gifts. "I'll take this big square box here, I guess." He unwrapped it and pulled out a computer game called Pizza Parlor. "Hmm," was all he had to say when he saw it.

Mrs. Reg had a little more to say once she stopped laughing. "A computer game for you, Max?" she said. "You're lucky if you can find the button to turn the computer on."

"Thank you, Mother," Max said, rolling his eyes. "For your information, I've been practicing on Deborah's PC, and I'm almost computer literate. I'm sure I could figure out how to play this—uh—what exactly is the point of a game called 'Pizza Parlor,' anyway?"

"Oh, it's great, Max!" said Polly. "I've been dying to get it. You have to open and run your own computer pizza parlor. There are all kinds of obstacles you have to overcome, like rats and bad cheese and a mean landlord—"

"Sounds fascinating," Max interrupted. "But not for me. I'll trade with Stevie for that book."

Stevie willingly handed over *Advanced Training Methods*. She glanced at the computer game. It did look interesting. She doubted it was the gift that had been meant for her, but she wouldn't mind if she ended up with it.

Then Stevie stole a glance at Veronica. She was sitting

with her arms folded and a grumpy look on her face. The lump of coal was still sitting where she'd dropped it among the remains of the fancy Maxwell's paper. Stevie tried hard to hold back a grin. "Your turn, Lorraine," she said.

Lorraine chose a gift that Lisa knew well. It contained the currycomb and cat toy intended for Simon. Lorraine looked mystified when she opened it, but Simon began chuckling immediately. He glanced at The Saddle Club.

"Well, I don't know who this is meant for, but I don't think it's me," Lorraine said. "What's so funny, Simon?"

Simon tried to control himself. "Oh, nothing, Lorraine," he said. "But I think I know who it was meant for—me." He quickly described his experience with his sister's currycomb-loving cat.

Lorraine shrugged. "Well, in that case, it's all yours," she said. "Hand over the shirt." She held up the soccer T-shirt and looked it over. "Hmm, somehow this isn't quite my style. I'm going to make another trade," she declared. "This time I'll trade with Merrill."

Merrill passed Lorraine the socks and accepted the shirt in return.

"I'm not sure that shirt is Merrill's style, either, but hey, that's how this game goes," Stevie said. "Lisa, it's your turn."

Lisa picked up the largest of the remaining packages. "I'm not sure what this is, but it's such a strange shape I can't resist," she said. She unwrapped it. "A bullhorn?" Lisa held it up. It was a bright yellow plastic bullhorn with the words I'M THE BOSS! stamped on the side in large red letters. Lisa giggled. "This one's getting traded," she declared. "I think it's more appropriate for someone with a much bigger mouth than me."

Max gave her a suspicious look. The bullhorn was clearly intended for him, but it wasn't like Lisa to call him a big mouth.

Lisa smiled. "That's why I'm trading with Stevie," she said, reaching over to grab the computer game from Stevie's lap. "But that's not all," she added, pointing to Polly. "I'll take that film—I just finished my last roll."

"Great!" Polly exclaimed, happily taking the computer game from Lisa.

Joe was next. He eagerly ripped the paper off his package and found a baseball cap with HONORARY HORSE WISE MEMBER stitched on the front.

"Honorary?" he exclaimed, pretending to be shocked. "Is there something you're not telling me, Max? Am I being kicked out?"

"We voted you out, Joe," Stevie joked. "You're honorary from now on. Sorry you had to find out this way."

"Just for that, I'm going to trade with you, Stevie," Joe said, tossing the cap at her. "Let's see how you like being honorary."

Stevie lobbed the bullhorn at him. "Okay, then, you can be the resident big mouth for a while," she replied with a grin.

"Not for long," he replied. "I'm making another trade. There's no way I'm letting Merrill keep that soccer T-shirt. I've been wanting a World Cup shirt for ages."

Merrill passed him the shirt and took the bullhorn. "Does

this mean I get to be the stable big mouth?" she asked. Everyone laughed at that, including Merrill.

"My turn, my turn!" Carole exclaimed, bouncing up and down. There were only three gifts left in the pile now, and she grabbed one. "Boy, this is heavy," she commented as she unwrapped it. The gift turned out to be a crystal paperweight shaped like a soccer ball.

"Wow," Lisa commented when she saw it. The paperweight had clearly cost more than the ten dollars they were supposed to spend, and that could only mean one thing—it was from Veronica diAngelo.

Stevie rolled her eyes. If she hadn't known that Carole had picked Joe's name, she would have suspected that Veronica had bought the paperweight for him. So whom had she bought it for? Nobody else in the room was particularly interested in soccer, as far as she knew.

"I'm trading," Carole announced. "I've had my eye on that training book this whole time. Hand it over, Max."

"Is it finally my turn now?" Betsy asked. She took one of the two gifts that were left. It was small and thin. "Maybe it's money," she guessed hopefully as she slit open the paper and pulled out a thick sheet of paper. "Hey, almost," she said with a smile. She waved the paper. "It's a gift certificate for TD's."

Stevie sat up and looked at the gift certificate with interest. "Are you going to trade?" she asked Betsy.

Betsy nodded. "But not with you, Stevie. Sorry," she said. "I want those socks." She passed the gift certificate down to Lorraine.

"Okay, it's all up to you, Adam," Mrs. Reg said. "If you're happy with what you get, then everyone else is stuck with what they have."

"Oh, the pressure," Adam said, pretending to be nervous. He unwrapped the last gift—another paperback book. He looked at the cover with raised eyebrows. "Gee, I don't know if I should keep this or not," he said. "It looks pretty exciting." He held it up so everyone could see. It was a romance novel called *Summer Passions*.

Lorraine gasped when she saw it. "I didn't even know that was out in paperback yet!" she exclaimed excitedly.

Adam grinned. "In that case, let's trade, Lorraine," he said.

Lorraine tossed him the gift certificate and eagerly grabbed the book. "Cool!" she said. As she opened it, a bookmark fell out. "Hey, look, a bonus prize—a horse bookmark."

"No fair," Adam said. "I may have to trade back."

Lorraine clutched the book as if afraid he really meant it. "No way," she said. "I've been dying to read this. It's from you, isn't it, Polly?"

Her friend shook her head. "Nope," she said. "I didn't pick you."

"Are you finished, Adam?" Max asked.

"No way," Adam said. "I've got some more trading to do. This TD's gift certificate is tempting, but there's someone here who deserves it more than I do. So hand over that cap, Stevie." Once that trade was made, he turned to Merrill. "Your turn as the local big mouth is over, Merrill," he said. "But the good news is, you're now an official honorary member of Horse Wise."

Merrill accepted the cap happily and put it on. "Thanks," she said.

"You're welcome," Max replied, giving away who had bought the cap.

"I'm still not done," Adam said. "I'll trade this bullhorn for that paperweight, Max. Of course, it has nothing to do with your being a big mouth—I just want the paperweight."

"Nice save, Adam," Max said drily.

"I didn't know you liked soccer, Adam," Lorraine said.

Adam grinned as he took the paperweight from Max. "I don't," he said. "But my dad is a huge soccer freak, and his birthday is next week. This will make a nicer gift than anything I could afford. Thanks, whoever bought it."

"I did," Veronica said. She shot Adam a dirty look—she obviously hadn't wanted him to get it.

Then Veronica smiled sweetly at Joe. "It's just too bad that someone who really likes soccer didn't end up with it," she cooed.

Stevie gasped. Suddenly everything became clear to her. Veronica hadn't bought a gift for whoever she had chosen—she had bought one for Joe instead, trying to impress him! Stevie could hardly believe Veronica was willing to ruin the game for everyone by not playing by the rules. Luckily, everything had turned out okay despite her.

"Is that it, Adam?" Max asked. When the boy nodded, Max stood and spoke into his bullhorn. "Then I declare this Yankee Swap officially over. Everyone is stuck with what they got!"

Fortunately, everyone except Veronica was very happy with

the gift they ended up with. In fact, as people began to own up to who had bought what for whom, it turned out that everyone had ended up with the exact gift they were meant to. Lorraine had gotten the computer game for Polly, whose family had just bought a new computer. Joe had bought Lorraine the romance book—they were in the same study hall at school, and he had noticed her reading an earlier book by the same author instead of doing her schoolwork. Adam had bought Lisa the film and frame. Meg had chosen the training book for Carole. Polly had picked out the colorful socks for Betsy. And of course, Red had bought the TD's gift certificate for Stevie. "I figured that was easier than making you come and beg me for money every time," he said.

Stevie grinned. "That's for sure," she said. "And all this goes to show that our Yankee Swap worked out perfectly. Everyone got the gift that he or she deserved." She smiled sweetly at Veronica, who ignored her.

Instead, Veronica turned to Joe. "Is it time to start dancing yet?" she asked him pointedly.

Max overheard. "It sure is," he said. "Let's head back to the ring. Red has volunteered to play deejay for the evening, so if he's ready to go we can get this party started."

Stevie hurried back to the indoor ring with the others. She watched in annoyance as Veronica smiled flirtatiously at Joe. She had to do something. "Hey, Red," she called out. "I think we need a special first song. The birthday boy and the birthday girl should have the first dance together, don't you think?"

Red nodded and put on a slow song. Merrill started blushing furiously, but Joe stepped forward eagerly. "That's a great idea, Stevie," he said, offering Merrill his arm. "May I have this dance, Merrill?"

She nodded shyly, and they started dancing together. After a few seconds she stopped looking embarrassed and started looking happy.

When Stevie saw the look on Veronica's face as she watched the dancing couple, she was happy, too. And when Phil and A.J. arrived and Phil immediately hurried over to ask Stevie to dance, she knew things couldn't possibly get much better.

THE FOLLOWING MONDAY afternoon, Stevie, Carole, and Lisa were seated in their favorite booth at TD's. They had decided that using up Stevie's gift certificate from Red should be a Saddle Club project. They had just placed their orders with the waitress, who, as usual, had been horrified at Stevie's request: pistachio ice cream with black cherry and caramel toppings.

"I'm going to miss Merrill," Stevie commented, leaning back in her seat. "She was fun."

"Me too," Lisa said, taking a sip of water. "I have to admit I'm a little surprised you liked her so much, though, Stevie. She's so quiet and shy, and you're so . . . well . . . *not*."

"Oh, if I had a little more time I could cure her of that shyness thing entirely," Stevie said with a wave of her hand.

"Really?" Carole said skeptically. "I think we're lucky we helped cure her of her fears about jumping before she actually took Barq back with her to Maine."

"Speaking of Maine, do you think she was serious when she invited us to come visit her?" Stevie asked.

"I'm sure she was," Lisa said.

"Good," Stevie replied. "Because I'm already working on a foolproof plan to convince our parents to let us go . . ."

Carole ignored her. She turned to Lisa. "I hope Merrill keeps jumping," she said. "I think she could be really good with more practice."

"I think she'll keep it up. And I think she's grateful for what you did for her while she was here, even if she didn't quite know how to say that directly," Lisa said.

Carole nodded. "I could tell." She was silent for a moment. "I really would have missed Barq."

"We all would have," Lisa replied, and Stevie nodded.

"But he was there for her when he needed to be," Carole went on. "Barq, I mean. He helped her gain a little bit of confidence in herself."

"And then Belle and Prancer and Starlight and Teddy and Crystal helped her realize it," Lisa said.

"That's right," Carole said. "I guess it's just one more great thing horses can do for a person."

"That's for sure," Stevie said. "Although I don't know if the horses can take all the credit for one thing."

"What's that?" Lisa asked.

Stevie grinned. "The fantastic time Merrill had at the party on Saturday night. I think Joe Novick was at least partly responsible for that."

The others couldn't help but agree. Joe and Merrill had spent a lot of time dancing and talking together.

"Still, Merrill spent some time at the party with the other boys, too," Lisa reminded Stevie. "She's coming out of her shell a little—she never used to have anything to say to boys at all. But I don't think you can count her as one of the boy-crazy girls yet."

"Thank goodness," Stevie said fervently. "It just goes to show that she has enough sense to know there are more important things in life than boys and romance. Some *mature* people don't always seem to realize that."

Her friends knew she was referring to girls like Betsy and Veronica. Stevie had told them her theory about why Veronica had bought the expensive soccer paperweight, and they had agreed that it was one of the sneakier things Veronica had ever done in her long career as a sneak.

"Speaking of mature people," Stevie said, "what did you think of my great prank at the Yankee Swap?"

"Well . . . ," Carole paused and glanced over at Lisa. "To tell you the truth, I thought it was a little mean—"

"What?" Stevie interrupted, beginning to look annoyed.

But Carole hadn't finished. "Yes, it was a little mean—but much, *much* more creative than pouring sugar all over someone's stuff. In other words, it was pretty clever and definitely well-deserved, though maybe a little dangerous."

Stevie looked mollified. "Thanks. But what do you mean by

dangerous? I'm not afraid of the likes of Veronica diAngelo. She doesn't have a creative bone in her body."

"Revenge doesn't have to be creative to be unpleasant if you're on the receiving end," Lisa pointed out. "And you'll be receiving some from Veronica, unless I'm badly mistaken."

Stevie shrugged. "That doesn't scare me a bit," she declared. "In fact, I look forward to it. A quiet, predictable life without any surprises might be fine for someone shy and retiring like Merrill. But as for me, I like some excitement once in a while to spice things up."

Just then the waitress approached with their sundaes. She set them down without a word and left quickly.

Stevie picked up her spoon and took a big bite. "Mmm . . . ," she began, looking contented. But suddenly a horrified look crossed her face, and she started choking.

"Stevie!" Lisa cried. "Are you okay?"

"*Mmm!*" Stevie held a hand to her face, which was rapidly turning very red. She swallowed hard, then grabbed her glass of water and gulped it down without pausing. Then she grabbed Carole's glass and drank her water, too.

When every drop was gone, Stevie wiped her mouth with her hand and managed to gasp out, "H-hot sauce!"

"Huh?" Lisa asked.

But before Stevie could reply, a very smug-looking Veronica diAngelo stepped out from behind a nearby booth, one hand hidden behind her back. "Hello, Carole, Lisa," she said. "Hi there, Stevie. What's wrong? You look a little hot under the collar."

Stevie glared at her. "You!" she sputtered. "You did this, didn't you?"

Veronica pretended not to know what she was talking about for a moment. Then she broke into a smirk and pulled her hand out from behind her back. She was holding a bottle of triple-alarm hot sauce.

"Oh! I think there's been a terrible mistake," she said sweetly, glancing down at Stevie's dish. "It looks like you got *my* sundae by mistake—the super-spicy special." She gave an exaggerated shrug. "I guess the waitress must have *swapped* our orders."

She walked away without another word. At the look on Stevie's face, Carole and Lisa—faithful friends though they were—couldn't help themselves. They burst into laughter.

ABOUT THE AUTHOR

BONNIE BRYANT is the author of more than a hundred books about horses, including The Saddle Club series, Saddle Club Super Editions, the Pony Tails series, and Pine Hollow, which follows the Saddle Club girls into their teens. She has also written novels and movie novelizations under her married name, B. B. Hiller.

Ms. Bryant began writing The Saddle Club in 1986. Although she had done some riding before that, she intensified her studies then and found herself learning right along with her characters Stevie, Carole, and Lisa. She claims that they are all much better riders than she is.

Ms. Bryant was born and raised in New York City. She still lives there, in Greenwich Village, with her two sons.